The action brought Mike out of his black thoughts, and he moved with swiftness. He struck and struck again. All the stab wounds were to the stomach. King David screamed from the pain, and the more he twisted away, the more the boy stalked him. He screamed from sheer pain now, and as he fell, Mike bent down and plunged the knife into his prone figure. Blood ran over Mike's hands, and his clothes were covered with it. He struck King David one more time, high in the chest.

Books by Donald Goines

Black Gangster
Black Girl Lost
Crime Partners
Cry Revenge
Daddy Cool
Death List
Dopefiend
Eldorado Red
Inner City Hoodlum
Kenyatta's Escape
Kenyatta's Last Hit
Never Die Alone
Street Players
Swamp Man
White Man's Justice, Black Man's Grief
Whoreson

DONALD GOINES

NEVER DIE ALONE

KENSINGTON BOOKS
www.kensingtonbooks.com

HOLLOWAY HOUSE CLASSICS are published by
Kensington Publishing Corp.
119 West 40th Street
New York, NY 10018

ISBN-13: 978-1-4967-3326-9
ISBN-10: 1-4967-3326-6

First Kensington Trade Paperback Printing: December 2020

10 9 8 7 6 5 4 3 2 1

Printed in the United States of America

NEVER DIE
ALONE

1

PAUL PAWLOWSKI GLANCED around his dingy one-room flat and grinned. Well, ol' boy, he reflected with a cold, bitter humor, you've seen better times than this. Not that being stuck in the Upper West Side of New York City was too bad, just a damned nightmare.

It was a cold-water flat, with a small single bed occupying most of the room. An old beat-up dresser leaned on three legs against one wall, the fourth leg being an old telephone directory that someone had put underneath ages ago. The pages of the book had turned yellow from age, but at least it held the dresser firm.

Paul tossed his legs over the iron-framed bed and got up slowly. Raising his arms over his head, he stretched his six-foot-two frame, then ran his hands through his curly black hair. He stumbled over toward the sink and turned on the water.

There was no hot and cold faucet, only one faucet and only cold water came out of it. He made a face before shoving both hands under the water and tossing the chilly water back onto himself. The shock of the water completely awakened him.

"Now maybe I can act like a man," Paul said loudly, having long ago fallen into the habit of talking to himself. Removing an old comb with six of the teeth missing, Paul used it to fix his hair so that it wouldn't look as if he had just gotten out of bed.

He then went to work on his teeth, brushing them with an old yellow toothbrush that had seen better days. Satisfied with his morning toilet, Paul removed a clean white shirt from the dresser and laid it out on the bed. Pulling back the mattress, he removed a pair of black pants that he had placed there the night before. It was the system he used to press his pants, wrapping the legs in newspapers, then placing them under the mattress. It was a cheap way to take the wrinkles out. After checking the pants to make sure they were wrinkle free, Paul removed some clean socks from the dresser and placed them next to the other clothes on the bed. His shorts were hanging on a hanger over the sink. He removed the freshly washed underwear from the hanger, and then he placed them on the bed.

Paul checked his watch to make sure he wasn't running late for his appointment. It was just 11:30. He still had an hour and a half to kill. He debated on whether or not he should take a bath, but since the bathtub was down the hall next to the second-floor toilet, he decided against taking one. One of these days, he promised himself, I'm going to have me an apartment with a bath and private toilet right there for my personal use.

Just to kill more of the extra time he had on his hands, Paul began to wash up in the sink, making sure he scrubbed thoroughly under his arms. When he finished, he reached for the can of deodorant on the wooden shelf over the sink. He cursed loudly as he shook the can and found it empty. "Next time I sell another short story I'm going to buy me at least two fuckin' cans of the shit," he promised himself.

But then he remembered that he was going on an interview for a job, and that he might not have to wait for his next royalty check from his publishers for his two paperback books. A writer's life was pure hell, he reflected. Sometimes he had a few extra dollars, in March or September when his royalty checks arrived. But the other months were hell, unless the writer happened to be a good money manager. But to find a writer who could manage money was rare, because anyone who was adept at it would also have enough common sense to pick a better livelihood.

As Paul began to dress with care, he glanced in the tiny mirror over the dresser. Shaggy brows and bright, friendly blue eyes glared back at him. He ran his hand over the well-trimmed Van Dyke beard as he gravely scrutinized the large Jewish nose that revealed his true heritage.

Even though Paul was Polish, his mother had been Jewish, something he was deeply proud of. Even as he glanced in the mirror, old memories that he tried to keep buried began to awaken. The day in Germany when his father had welcomed his mother's parents to their house. He had made him move across the street to his uncle's home under the pretext that his grandparents needed his room.

At the time Paul didn't understand it, being just twelve years old, but he felt something was wrong. In the past, whenever his grandparents came to visit, they had always stayed in the guest room, never needing Paul's bedroom. But on this occasion Paul was told to move and not to come across the street until one of his parents came over after him.

1938, the year that Paul saw the German soldiers come and put the yellow Star of David on the front door. It wasn't until much later that Paul realized that his father could have escaped the madness that came their way, but he had stayed right beside his wife. Paul never found out what really happened to his parents and grandparents, but he liked to believe that his father was allowed to stay beside the woman he loved until the very last moment. It was a romantic thought, but one that he cherished deeply.

The day after the truck came and took his parents and grandparents, Paul's uncle made the necessary arrangements and before Paul knew what was happening he found himself in Paris.

Until he was eighteen, Paul spent his years in boarding schools.

His uncle had died before the end of the war, so Paul was left on his own rather early in life. The little bit of money that came out of Germany to him was spent on his education. Before his college days were over, Paul had had to find a job to help finish his education.

"Now," he said grimly into the mirror, "you Jewish Polack bastard, let's get on uptown and overwhelm those cocksuckers with your grand nobility."

Paul slipped on his suit coat, took one more glance in the mirror, then brushed off some imaginary dust from the lapel of the dark sport coat. He adjusted the black tie he had put on for the occasion and made ready to depart.

One quick glance down at his shoes made him hesitate. He took a quick look at his watch, then hurried over to the dresser and searched around under the shirts and shorts until he found an old T-shirt. He examined the shirt carefully before deciding to use it to wipe off his shoes. He took out some polish and quickly applied some to the toe of each shoe. Using an old brush he got out of the top drawer, he brushed the shoes carefully. When he finished, the shoes shined expertly. It was always this way when he worked, never wasting a moment, and not spending much time.

Spring was in the air. Paul could smell it as he raised his head like a hound dog on the hunt. Even here in New York a man could smell the freshness of spring. Some of the gutters still held dirty water from the ice that had melted long ago. The water didn't have anywhere to drain off to because the drains were still plugged from the trash of last fall.

It was only down in the ghetto that a person encountered such neglect. Here, on 87th Street between Broadway and Amsterdam, the blacks, poor whites, and spics were trapped in their own private prison. Some would never rise up out of the poverty that surrounded them. The lucky ones would eventually earn enough money from selling drugs, or have the money their women would earn, to leave. Yet most of them wouldn't move because they were frightened of the outside world. This was the only world they knew—the slums, with the hustlers and bums falling over each other. So they would live and die in their ghetto, afraid of the outside.

Paul waved to the elderly black man who sold newspapers on the corner. The man waved back as Paul went by. Peddlers moved up and down the street, calling out at customers and friends alike, so that there was a constant cacophony of voices. A visitor touring through these parts would many times be lost and frightened by the strange sounds coming up from the bowels of the city.

Paul reached the subway and ran down the steps quickly, taking two at a time. A train had come in, but there was no hurry. Another one would come roaring through in less than five minutes.

After paying his fare, Paul hurried on, reaching the train before the doors closed. He jumped into the second car, right before the doors began to close. It took less than ten minutes before Paul was downtown. He made his way out of the subterranean station and found 54th Street. Removing a small piece of paper from his pocket, he studied the address carefully, then folded the paper neatly and put it in his pocket.

The sidewalks were crowded with people. Again Paul wondered idly just where all these people could be going. Every time he came downtown he was overwhelmed by the crowds. Even at night the streets and sidewalks were jammed with people, most of them seeming to be in a hurry to get wherever it was they were going.

Paul almost passed by the building he was searching for. He back-stepped a few paces, then entered the dingy-looking building. He stepped in the lobby and examined the directory on the far wall. He ran his fingers down the names of the occupants until he found what he was looking for. *The Evening Star* was at the bottom of the list.

The large lobby led to three elevators. Paul took the first one and punched the button for the fourth floor. He wondered if the rest of the elevators were as dilapidated as the one he was using. The elevator moved slowly upward, cranking loudly. Paul raised his eyes toward heaven as if in prayer, then noticed the escape door in the ceiling. He speculated on how an elderly person would go about getting out in an emergency. He would be hard pressed himself to reach the escape door, even with his height. He'd have to jump and pull himself upward with just his arms—something that many men in their prime couldn't do, let alone an old man or woman.

For the first time since applying for the job, Paul wondered if it would even come close to his expectations. The sight of the building killed some of the joy he'd had. His asking price dropped lower before he even got off the elevator. But, he reminded himself, the man he had talked to over the telephone, Mr. Billings, had made it sound interesting. Mr. Billings had read Paul's two novels and believed he was just the man they were looking for to write a by-line in the weekly newspaper.

Paul wished he'd done his homework better. Instead of buying a newspaper and seeing what kind of copy *The Evening Star* put out, he'd given up after trying to find the paper at only two newsstands. He'd postponed getting one because he would have had to go uptown. Now he regretted his laziness. Mr. Billings had mentioned that the paper did lean slightly toward the left. But what the hell did that mean? Right or left, what damn difference did it make?

The elevator door opened slowly, and Paul stepped forward to see what his future held.

2

KING DAVID, BETTER KNOWN as "King Cobra" when he wasn't around, took one more glance at the street map of New York City and tossed it into the glove compartment. He started the engine of the Cadillac and pulled out into the traffic. It had been five years since he left New York City— but now he was returning, and in all his glory.

The dark green mohair suit fitted King David well. He was a small-built man and thus wore his clothes well. Even with his· high-heeled black ox-fords, his height barely reached five-foot-nine.

King David began to feel that warm, good feeling as he neared the city. When he had left, he was only a black man running with just the clothes on his back. He'd managed to cheat certain people out of nice sums of money to help him travel. And that was the first thing he'd have to take care of, he reflected, as he reached over and pushed his cigarette lighter in. He would have to make sure he paid off his debts, so that there wouldn't be any trouble.

For a brief moment the bushy eyebrows came together as he frowned. The sharp, birdlike eyes set deep in the dark brown face grew large with fear as he remembered that Moon, the neighborhood dope man, was one of the people he had ripped off for a nice piece of money. King David didn't need to be told that he had left behind an enemy that would never forget, but King David believed the man was greedy enough to be bought off. With the fifty thousand dollars he had stashed away in the trunk of the car, he was sure he could satisfy Moon. A small piece of that stash would do the trick, he thought coldly. He had only beat Moon for five hundred dollars, so a thousand dollars would clear the air between them. Neither man really wanted any trouble, King David kept telling himself. Moon couldn't stand it, not in his business. Their way of life depended on them staying out of the Man's sight, so quite naturally he believed Moon would jump at the chance to gain back twice as much money as he lost.

Whether or not he would make good the money he took from the women who had believed in him was another matter altogether. He couldn't see how any of them could bring him trouble that he couldn't handle, so he might just save money there. After all, this wasn't Christmas, and he damn sure wasn't Santa Claus.

King David pulled up at the end of the line behind the rest of the cars waiting to cross the Brooklyn Bridge. He waited patiently until it was his turn to pay his toll. As he drove away from the toll station he knew that the only thing ahead of him now was that bridge that led into New York City. "You're just about home, baby," he sang out loudly as he pushed the gas pedal down to the floor, causing the Cadillac to leap forward.

Within an hour, King David was pulling up in front of the Blue Room bar on Broadway. He entered the dimly lit nightclub and stood in the lobby until his eyes became adjusted to the dark. Then he made his way over to the bar.

"Well, look what the dogs have dug up!" Jasper Williams yelled from behind her bar. She was a tall, light-skinned dyke who could dress up and look damn good whenever she wanted to, but most of the time she preferred to dress like a man.

"Honey," she said as King David came up to the bar, "I heard you had went down to the Big Foot country and decided to stay there for your health. Now, with spring coming, here you are. It sure means we goin' have one hot-ass summer around here!"

"Hi, Jasper," King David said as he slid onto a barstool. "Things can't be that bad. I thought folks would miss me around here."

Jasper glanced closely at him to see if he was serious, then laughed loudly like a man. "Nigger, you must be insane. Ain't nobody ever missed a rattlesnake if it wasn't in their bed when they got ready to go to sleep, so how in the hell could they possibly miss you?"

"Aw, baby, you ain't got to be that cold, have you?" King David inquired in the little boy's voice that he used for con action.

The tall woman looked down her nose at him. "Nigger, don't come down on me with that weak-ass shit of yours. I know all the people who were looking for you when you split, and as of now, I believe some of them will be damn glad to hear about you showing back up!"

For a second, a chill flashed through King David, but he quickly shook it off. If he handled everything like he had planned, it would work out. "Tell me something, Jasper, is Moon still around?"

"Uh-huh, and I'll bet he'd be willing to pay a nice sum just to know how you're doing. In fact," Jasper continued, "I'll bet he's one of the most interested people in your health and whereabouts."

David shook off the feeling of dread. "How can I get in touch with him? I got some bread for him."

Jasper grinned. "Now how about that! I would never have believed a good con man like you would be trying to pay back some of the people you ripped off!"

"I'm not interested in what you think or believe, Jasper. If you want to make this fifty-dollar bill, you'll figure out some way to get him on the phone so that I can rap with him."

The woman stared down at the money for a minute, then snatched it up. She walked down to the end of the bar and removed a telephone.

As King David watched her in silence, he sipped the drink she had left him. He hadn't bothered to order. She remembered that he only drank gin and Squirt.

Jasper glanced up as she began to talk into the receiver. "Hello, Moon. This is Jasper over at the Blue Room. Yeah, I think I got somebody here you might be interested in talking to."

The man on the other end of the line spoke sharply into the telephone. Jasper decided to make the call fast, because she didn't want to get involved any further. "Man, I didn't mean to disturb you, but I thought you'd like to know that King Cobra is here. Yeah, you know who I mean, King David. He wants to say a few words to you."

The other end of the line went silent for a minute. She thought Moon had hung up. Then the man's voice came over sharp and clear. "Put the nigger on. I got a few things to say to him."

Jasper waved for King David to come down and pick up the phone. As far as she was concerned, she had made a fast fifty dollars.

King David took his time as he walked down to the phone. Things weren't working out as he had planned. He wasn't making the big splash he had intended to make, and it was all because of this smartass bitch behind the bar. He wanted her to see that he wasn't in any hurry.

Jasper watched him come down the bar, trying to walk so coolly. The bastard won't be so jazzy when Moon and his boys finish with his ass, she thought.

Still taking his time, King David picked up the phone. "What's happenin', baby?" he asked. "Long time since I talked to you."

"You're damn right it's been a long time!" Moon answered sharply. "I don't know what brings you back to the city, but I'd guess you must have my fuckin' money."

"Yeah, baby, I got your paper, so don't get in any uproar. Everything is goin' be all right."

Moon hesitated for a minute. "I hope you realize that, since it's been this long, there's some interest on that damn money."

This was what David had been waiting for. "Aw man, I ain't rich, baby, but I can dig where you're coming from. How much extra money am I supposed to come up with?"

While David had been talking, Moon had been trying to remember how much money the punk owed him. "Yeah, King Cobra, I know you ain't rich, but I also know you must have my paper or you wouldn't be talking to me." Moon snapped his fingers, then said slowly, "You hold on a minute, David, I want to check my books. I got you wrote down somewhere."

Without waiting for a reply, Moon lay down the

receiver and walked into his bedroom. He sat on the edge of the king-sized bed and opened up the drawer. The small nightstand beside the bed had its twin on the other side. Each nightstand had a statue of a black woman rising from the base, leading up to the top of the lamp. Heavy black drapes covered the window so that there was no chance of anyone seeing in from the outside.

Moon flipped through the pages of his record book quickly, using the index. Not finding what he wanted under the name "David," he then looked under the letter "S" for snakes. Not finding it there, he sat back and rubbed his double chin. Moon was a heavyset black man who had once been powerfully built. The muscles had turned to fat from easy living. His eyes were almost covered by the layers of fat that rolled over his body. A heavy black, bushy beard with sideburns that met his whiskers encircled large and extremely red lips. He wore a natural that was thinning rapidly with age. But everything about the man was overpowered by the little pig eyes that stared out from his massive face. The evil that he possessed was revealed by those eyes. Nothing but heavy black shades could camouflage that look in his eyes.

Again Moon snapped his fingers, then looked under "C" for Cobra. He ran his fingers down the few names and a slight smile broke through his heavily bearded lips as he found what he was looking for.

"Yeah, my man," Moon said, picking up the receiver. "From my books it's like you owe me six hundred big ones from the bell." He fell silent, waiting to see if King David would say anything about the extra hundred he had tacked on.

"Damn!" David cursed. "From my books it wasn't but five hundred dollars, my man."

"Yeah, well, that's not the problem anyway," Moon stated coldly. "We ain't took into consideration the interest on the six hundred, you know what I mean?" This time Moon didn't wait for David's answer. "Now over five years have passed and that's a lot of interest."

"Okay, Moon, I didn't call you to argue, I just want to straighten up the books with you so that I won't have any problems, you dig?"

"Yeah, I dig right where you're coming from," Moon replied. "So let's do it like this, Dave. You give my boys a grand when they show up. I figure that should cover whatever trouble I've gone through trying to locate you so that I could get my money or some of your ass."

For a minute, King David's temper got the best of him, but he controlled it enough so that the man on the other end of the telephone didn't realize it. It was just what he had figured Moon would ask for, so there was no problem. Anyway, it was worth the money to pay up so he wouldn't have any trouble.

"Okay, Moon, I'll pay it. I just want you to call off your dogs; is that a deal?"

"Yeah, baby, if something happens to you, it won't be because you owe me any money."

"That's just mellow, Moon," David replied. Then he couldn't help but brag a little. "Have your boys meet me at the Blue Room. My new Caddie is parked across the street, so more than likely I'll be sittin' in it, watching the traffic going and coming."

Moon laughed. "You ain't got to worry, King. Anytime a man calls and offers me a grand, he gets the best treatment of the house." He laughed again and hung up, not waiting for David's reply.

Moon walked out of his bedroom and into the living room. He looked at the young men lounging around in the plush room. A couple were bodyguards, the others were his closest pushers, the only men that Moon sold dope to.

Moon pointed the small book at the young black man across the room. "Mike," he began, "I think a friend of yours has come back to town."

The well-dressed young man in his early twenties raised the glass of scotch whiskey in his hand and downed it. "From the phone call I could figure it out a little," Mike said, setting the empty glass on the bar behind him.

Wall-to-wall carpeting, a gold couch and a marble coffee table with matching end tables spelled only a portion of Moon's success.

"Tell me, Mike," Moon said, lowering himself onto his favorite gold love seat, "I sort of forget what it was he did to you. It might not be important enough for you to go to the trouble you're going to have to go through to play payback."

"Ain't no amount of trouble enough to stop me

from killin' that motherfucker," Mike stated bitterly.

Moon watched the young man closely; he knew it wasn't any idle threat. Mike was young, but he was dangerous. He was a professional killer with just his hands. A black belt in karate gave a man that power. But more than likely, killing King David would force him to use someone else.

"Well, I guess you know I gave him my word that I wouldn't be involved in any trouble coming his way. Though I haven't forgotten the embarrassment that came my way after the word got out that punk had played on me and got away."

Mike got up and went around the bar so that he could fix himself another drink. He waited until he was finished before speaking. Leaning on the bar, he glanced around at his friends. Killing a man was something you didn't do lightly, and the fewer people who knew about it the better off the killer was.

The other men in the room stared back at the tall Negro. "If you think you're going to need any help, Mike, you can count on me."

Mike stared at the jet black man. He was so dark he had gained the nickname "Blue" in his younger days. He was slender and supple, all bone and muscle, with a brutal leanness about his face. His skin was so dark it had a shine about it, matching the startling black eyes that had the look of the hunter. There was no humor in them.

Mike glanced at his best friend. "I was counting

on you, Blue, but I'm glad you offered your help so I didn't have to ask for it."

"Good, good," Moon said, "now maybe we can hear what it's all about?"

It was obvious that Mike didn't want to repeat the tale, but his boss wasn't leaving him any choice. Moon's word was law. Either you did what he said or found somewhere else to work, if you were lucky enough to get away with a whole skin.

There was anguish in the young man's voice as he began to speak. "I was fifteen when it happened, man. I thought I was a man, but King Cobra proved to me that I was just a young punk." Visualizing the scene again, Mike's face tightened up in anger. "My mother had just got her county check, you know, and it was eight of us in the house to feed. Well, King David waited until the insurance man came by and cashed the check, then he took it from her. Every motherfuckin' penny. He tossed her ten fuckin' dollars out of a three-hundred-dollar check. I guess he meant for us to try and live on it. Anyway, I charged at the bastard, but I didn't have anything in my hand. At the same time, he had been sipping on a Coke, keeping the bottle for protection, in case anything went wrong."

Mike paused and shifted nervously. "My mother reached for the nigger before I did, but he fired a straight right to her head, and it took her out of the picture. Next in line was me. He used the Coke bottle." Mike opened his mouth, revealing the gap where his two front teeth were missing. "This is what I got out of my funky attempt to help my momma, but I ain't never forgot."

The story had been short and to the point. Now the other two gunmen in the room shifted around nervously. It was one thing to be all right with a guy and quite another to swear to help him kill a nigger when nothing was to be gained. They could understand Mike's anger, but they were too callous to be really moved. All except Blue, that is. The spectacle of wiping out a punk fascinated him. In reality, he enjoyed killing. It was only then that he really felt alive.

"We don't need these motherfuckers' help, Mike," Blue stated in a chilling voice. There was no doubt in anyone's mind whether or not he meant it. His eyes glittered dangerously. The other men were too aware of Blue; they could tell when he was aroused. The killer was beginning to breathe heavily.

Finally, Moon made his decision. "Now Mike, behind me giving my word, this is how it's goin' have to be done. Rockie and Alvin will go and pick up my grand, then you and Blue can move in and do your thing." Moon stopped and pointed his finger as if it were a gun. "I mean it, boys, don't do nothing to blow my grand. After that, I could care less."

Rockie grinned at Mike. "When do we get started?"

"Right now," Moon said as his two gunmen stood up. "Ain't no reason why we should let that money sit by when all you have to do is pick it up, so get started. He'll be sittin' in his new Cadillac across the street from the Blue Room."

As the two well-dressed men started for the door, Mike walked over and picked up the phone. He made his call quickly. "Sis," he said sharply, "I want you to be downstairs waiting for me. It's important. Oh yeah, baby, be sure to put on your shortest mini. We need you to catch the attention of someone."

Before the woman could reply, Mike hung up the phone. Moon grinned at him. "She's kind of young to be using on a job like this, ain't she?"

"She wasn't too young to see her mother get the shit kicked out of her on more than one occasion," Mike replied sharply.

"Okay," Moon said quietly. "You guys are on your own. If something funky goes down, don't involve me. I don't want no parts of it, you dig?"

Neither man answered as they walked swiftly toward the door. It was too late for words now; action was the only thing left.

3

THE ELEVATOR STOPPED on the fourth floor and Paul Pawlowski stepped out into the dimly lit hallway. He didn't have any trouble finding his way to the newspaper office. They occupied the entire floor. Taking a chance, Paul opened the first door he came to.

The receptionist glanced up from her desk as Paul walked toward her. He tried to smile, but could feel it frozen on his face. "Yes, could I help you?" she inquired in a voice that sounded better than she looked. She was small with tiny breasts revealed by a see-through blouse. Her face was made up heavily, with her hair dyed a bright blonde.

Paul wondered idly if she could be real. He couldn't see her legs, but he would have bet money that they were small. Everything about her represented a woman on the make. As he stood in front of her, she allowed her eyes to run up and down his body. For a second he felt like a prize bull about to be sold.

He cleared his throat. "I'm supposed to have an appointment with Mr. Billings, miss."

"Miss Levern Harding, dear. But you can call me Levern, if you care to."

"Okay, Levern, but now how about Mr. Billings? I'm supposed to have a one o'clock appointment with him," Paul stated a little more coldly than he meant to. But the woman was coming on just too strong—something he couldn't stand in his women. He liked to be the one who did the chasing, not the other way around.

The woman pouted her lips, then picked up the phone and called Mr. Billings. "Okay, honey, he will see you now. It's the first office on your right."

It wasn't hard to find. The offices were nothing but rooms partitioned off with the cheapest of plywood. Paul hesitated in front of the office he took to be Mr. Billings', then raised his hand and knocked softly.

"Come in, come on in," the voice from inside the office roared out good-naturedly.

Paul pushed the door open and stepped in. The first thing he noticed was the huge fat man sitting behind an old beat-up desk. The man had thinning gray hair with blond eyebrows. His lips were twisted in a cruel sneer that seemed to be part of him, no matter how good-natured he acted. Across his upper lip was one of the largest handlebar mustaches Paul had ever seen. Can this crap be for real? Paul wondered as he stared around. The rest of the office was bare, except for two beaten-up chairs that sat in front of the desk. It didn't look as if the company was too profitable.

The big man stood up and stretched out his hand. "How do you do, Mr. Pawlowski, I've been waiting for you."

Paul nodded his head. Interviews always made him nervous. "About that editing job, Mr. Billings, am I right when I say you mentioned something about a by-line?"

"Yes, yes indeed. A by-line goes along with it. I hope you don't mind me calling you 'Paul.' It breaks the ice a little if we're on a first-name basis. And you can call me 'John.' "

Paul cleared his throat and waited for John to let him in on what he was supposed to do. "Uh, John," the first name gave him a little trouble, but he managed to get it out, "what kind of by-line am I supposed to write?"

John beamed down at him before returning to his seat. "You're a man after my own heart, Paul. Yes sir, indeed. You like to come right to the point, as I can see."

Paul waited, wondering when the man *was* going to get to the point. There was something wrong, but he couldn't put his finger on it.

"Now Paul, there's one thing you should know. Most of our papers sell in the South. It's our biggest outlet, so we have to sort of slant our work toward the southern white, you know what

I mean." Billings let out a big laugh, and Paul knew if he had been standing next to the man, the fat bastard would have probably slapped him on his back.

"No, I don't think I quite know what you mean, Mr. Billings. When you say slant our work toward the southern white, I'm at a slight loss understanding just what you mean."

"It's not hard," Billings answered, smiling broadly. "I read your last novel, and that part you had in there about that big black buck raping three white women before he was caught. That's the stuff I'm talking about. My southern readers will eat it up."

Paul was too dumbfounded to answer. He just stared at the fat man. Billings took his silence to mean he went along with the idea. "Now, if you can lay that kind of crap on thick enough, hell, we'll sell every copy."

The surprise left Paul. Now he was only numb. "That happened to be a novel, not a news story. It was fiction, not real life. I used a black character because the book called for one. It made it more real. I didn't do it to make people in the South happy; I just wrote a novel, and it didn't sell that damn well."

"Now, now," Billings said lightly. "The work I have for you won't have to be fiction. There's enough rape going on in Harlem so that you don't have to make up a fuckin' thing, Paul. All you have to do is spread the truth a little. You know, dig the dirt up, that's what sells."

"Paul," Billings continued, "there's money in this kind of crap, I wouldn't shit you about it. In less than a month, you'll be living like a king. All you have to do is dig." Billings was so involved in what he was saying that he didn't pay any attention to Paul's face. It was becoming red as a beet.

"Now Paul, there's one more thing that will sell like hell down south. Toss a little crap in that by-line about Jews, you know. The Jews up this way are constantly causing the niggers to try and be more than they are. We build on these two concepts, and I promise you, buddy, you'll get a raise before you know it."

"Don't call me buddy!" Paul stated, trying to control his anger. His fists were clenched so tightly the knuckles were white. "I guess you want something like what Hitler did, a lot of raving about how dirty the Jews are and that kind of shit."

Billings broke out smiling. "That's it! We write about parties the Jews went to with the jigs, having their women dancing with the black bastards and all that shit. I tell you, boy, it will really sell. I know what I'm talking about. I've been in this business for years."

"I guess that's the only reason why your fuckin' paper sells only in the South. It's pure dirt, Billings." For the first time Billings stopped talking and glanced up from his desk. He didn't like the look on the young man's face. If he could read minds, he wouldn't have liked the thoughts going through the young man's mind at all.

Paul was seeing Germany all over again, seeing the men with the black shirts yelling at the crowds about the "dirty Jews." Rabble-rousers from the word go, but their shouting and screaming finally paid off. People had listened, then turned their heads when the killings began. It was this kind of man who was responsible for his mother and father being dead. Men who didn't care who was hurt, just as long as they made their blood money for the lies they told.

Billings read something threatening in Paul's face. "If you don't like to write about the Jews, that's okay," he added quickly. "I've got another man on the staff who can handle that part of it. All you'll have to do is dig up crap about the jigs. We can sell anything you write, as long as you make it strong enough."

Paul stood up and leaned over the desk, bracing himself on the palms of his hands. "First of all, Billings, there's something I think you should know. I'm Jewish myself. Don't let the Polish name fool you. My mother was all Jewish, and I'm damn proud of being of that race. Secondly, I feel sorry for blacks. I live in a building with some of the tenants being black, so I know what kind of hell they catch without a bastard coming along trying to make money off of lies printed about them.

"Third, I think the South has enough problems without me writing something that would inflame some ignorant bastard so that he got drunk and took out his anger on some poor black bastard who doesn't have the slightest idea of why it's happenin' to him. Next, and last, this is what I think about you and your idea." With that, Paul leaned over and spat in the man's face. "Now, you can do any goddamn thing you think you're big enough to do, if you don't like what I did."

Before Billings could answer, Paul spun around on his heel and walked out the door. He was so mad that he ignored the woman as she smiled brightly at him. His face was red as a beet. He fumbled with the elevator, impatiently pushing the button until the car finally arrived. He shoved his way into the empty elevator and rode down to the lobby.

His rage was still growing as he came out onto the street. He walked blindly until he found a bar that had a "three for one" sign up. He went in and began to get fairly drunk, not bothering to worry about the grocery money he was drinking up. "I wish I could have kicked the bastard in his fat ass," Paul murmured angrily.

"What did you say, mac?" another customer asked from the stool next to him.

"Nothing," Paul replied harshly, the tone of his voice revealing that he was in the wrong mood to be tampered with.

The man on the next stool was too wise to follow it up. He had been drinking in bars in New York for years, so he knew when to leave well enough alone. The shadows began to get large outside, but Paul didn't notice. He continued to drink, trying to figure out what kind of fucking world it was that he lived in.

A bastard like Billings would go home to his fat wife and big house, with the green grass in front of it, while Paul would end up climbing the stairs to his second-floor flat with the cold water. But at least he was a man with some kind of scruples. If he had to live in a cold-water flat the rest of his days, he'd do it before he sold his manhood. And that's just what a job with Billings' paper would be, selling out his manhood for a soft job. Better to starve than live off the misfortune of others.

It was dark when Paul staggered from the bar. He had spent his food money and had to leave. But it had been enough to get him totally smashed. He didn't go in for heavy drinking too often, but when he did he went the limit.

As Paul staggered down the street, he had to ask directions to the subway. Many of the people he approached hurried and got out of his way, not bothering to try to hear what he was saying. To them, he was just another ghetto drunk, possibly dangerous if they didn't watch their step around him. Nobody knew what a drunkard might do, and they weren't taking any chances.

Finally, Paul got a young boy to point out the way to the nearest subway. It was in the next block. Paul made his way to it and went down the steps. Since he was still uptown he didn't have to worry too much about the gangs of tough youths that roamed the streets searching for drunks. But when he reached his neighborhood his danger would increase unless he straightened up. The night air did him good. Even though it was spring, the evening breeze was rather chilly. The cool air sobered him up enough so that when he got off the subway, he could walk without staggering all over the street.

When he reached his street and started up it, he saw some men arguing with each other. Then he heard a man scream. The scream was repeated over and over again.

Paul started running toward them. "What the hell's going on there?" he hollered as he neared the struggling threesome.

At the sight of Paul, two of the men broke away and ran toward a car parked across the street. Paul noticed from the light of the streetlamp that a young girl sat behind the steering wheel. As soon as the men entered the car, it sped rapidly away.

As Paul neared the man they had been struggling with, the man crumpled up and fell to the pavement.

4

AFTER HANGING UP the telephone, King David walked back down the length of the bar and ordered another drink from Jasper.

"You don't look too happy there, King," Jasper stated as she set the drink in front of him.

King David glanced at her coldly. "You need something to do, bitch, then you might worry about your own business. I don't need no help in taking care of mine." He stopped and gestured along the bar. "Give everybody on the bar what they want. Since you ain't got no help back there, it will keep you out of my face for a while!"

She glanced down the bar, already aware that it was semi-full. "You black bastard," she said loud enough for the nearest customers to hear.

The tone of voice she used angered him. "Simple ass, do your job and give everybody a drink," King David roared. The whole bar heard him.

When she hesitated and put her hands on her hips, two young dappers yelled from the middle of the bar. "Quit bullshittin', woman, and take care of this white man's bar! If he was here, you'd be running up and down like a track star!"

Jasper opened her mouth but quickly closed it, making her look like a fish out of water. Her yellow cheeks became red as she fought back the anger, and common sense prevailed. Jasper had worked the bar too long. She had spent too many years working around blacks. Black men were quick to kill, and sometimes their moods were already down on them before they ever reached the bar.

So she turned on the charm instead of the anger. She flashed her teeth and hustled down to the young men. "What's wrong with you niggers tonight? Can't pick up no bitches?"

Both the young boys smiled at her. Since she was waiting on them first, they didn't have to worry about the stud at the end of the bar changing his mind. "Hey baby, we just ain't got all night to wait on a drink. One of our ladies might be down and we'd have to leave right away."

"Yeah, baby," the other brother said after his friend stopped. "It ain't that we're hustling drinks either. It's just that we like to drink along with any hip brothers who's handling big enough to run 'em up and down the bar."

"Okay, baby," Jasper answered. "I know both of you are big spenders too. Now what would you like? Another beer like what you got or something more expensive?"

The smaller of the two partners frowned, caus- ing the thin razor scar on the side of his dark brown cheek to look like a straight line. He knew she had put them down, but it had been done lightly. They lived in the neighborhood and came to the bar every day, sometimes in the mornings, sitting around joking with the white owner who worked the day shift. They accepted Jasper's tongue, because she always steered them to drunken tricks that had found their way to the bar for the first time. Whenever they pulled a rip-off, she would be waiting with her hand out, and they always argued over the money.

"Naw, baby," the light-brown-skinned brother said. "Give us some scotch whiskey, double, over the rocks." He made a fist of black power, and raised his hand in the air toward King David.

The King raised his glass in reply. He knew as well as the boy who did it that it meant nothing. The boy was wondering how hard it would be to take King David's bankroll, and as Jasper leaned over and poured the drinks, he put his thoughts to work.

"Say, baby, that nigger down there seems to have plenty of that green shit. He might not talk so loud if somebody removed some of it." He looked at his partner to see if they were thinking the same way.

"Daddy Cool," she said to the lightest one, "you

35

NEVER DIE ALONE

and Littl' Bro had better stay clear of that nigger. That's King Cobra down there, and since he's a small nigger, he carries a great big pistol."

"King Cobra," Littl' Bro said coldly. "Who the fuck is King Cobra?"

Daddy Cool laughed loudly but kept his voice down. If the man was really dangerous, and any nigger with a gun was dangerous, it was best the man didn't know they were discussing him.

"His name is King David, honey," Jasper explained quickly. "Don't too many people call him King Cobra to his face. He don't like to be called a snake, but he sure in the fuck is one." Before they could tie her up with questions, she added, "Him and Moon got something up, so that might give you an idea of whose ballpark you might end up playing in if you get involved with him." She left them then, knowing that they would think about what she had said.

Mentioning Moon was the quickest way to stop them from plying her with questions. Even though they now knew that King David carried a gun, that hadn't stopped them from thinking about ways to knock him off. The mention of Moon's name, however, would take all the desire out of thinking about ripping him off.

Jasper moved on up the bar, filling drinks without inquiring about what kind they wanted. Whatever was sitting in front of them was what they got. To an inquiry about who sent the drink, she would just nod in King David's direction. Every-

36

body knew who was buying, but some of the lone women wanted to know his name.

After receiving her new drink, Lady Bird, an old customer of the bar who hustled the customers, picked up her drink and started down the bar in King David's direction. Lady Bird had been working the streets of New York for over twenty years. She had started when she was fourteen and had picked up the nickname "Lady" because she walked so daintily. Over the years she had become fleshy to the point of chubbiness, and her face, though noticeably young under the brazen whore make-up, appeared yellow and aged.

"Hi, honey," Lady Bird chirped in a high voice. The reason they called her "Bird" was very evident when she spoke. Her voice was high to the point of being shrill, sometimes grating the nerves and becoming tiresome.

When King David was hustling, he would have loved to be approached by a woman like Lady Bird. He'd end up getting her money if he had to take it at the point of his knife. But now, since he had all the money he needed for a while, he resented a woman like her trying to hustle him.

He twisted around on his barstool and stared at her as if something dirty had slithered from under the bar. It didn't take anything but a look, and Lady Bird knew she had made a mistake. "Excuse me, honey," she said quickly, running off to the ladies' room. She stopped at the jukebox and punched three records for a quarter.

When the soft jazz from the jukebox flooded the room, King David relaxed. He dreamed of the future. With his bankroll he could start backing his own numbers. Get a few runners to pick up for him, pay quickly and just make sure the runner delivered the hit money and his name would begin to ring. People talked about the number man who always paid as soon as the figures were right.

King glanced out the windows, which were heavily covered with posters of Miles Davis, Coltrane and Mose. It was evening. How different the time was from that back in Los Angeles he couldn't tell. The highway had made time irrelevant. Staying at motels whenever he felt like it, stopping over in Atlanta, Georgia, and visiting the beautiful club James Brown had built. It had been a good trip.

Now he was back, wondering why. He had hesitated in the South, the land drawing him to it. Build a cabin and go back to the land. But he had fought the urge. Remembering the many evenings in the cabin in Arizona, the lonely nights when he was a boy. The nearest people were the Indians on the reservation. The loneliness was something he'd never return to. This was his world, the dimly lit bars, the wheeling and dealing, where a fortune could be made overnight. Tax-free money, the kind the government never could get.

Three young girls entered, all of them wearing pants outfits. King David looked away. He was sick of seeing women in pants. It took something away from them. A woman in pants seldom drew his attention, unless she was of exceptional beauty.

He glanced at his watch. It was time he went out and waited on the pickup. It wouldn't be long, not the way Moon loved money. Shit, King reflected, it was Moon's greed that had cost him the five hundred in the first place.

King smiled as he remembered. It had only cost him twenty-five dollars to set it up. The first time he had spent his own two hundred giving it to Pig for the piece of heroin he bought. But the catch to it had been the white boy King had hired. He gave the white junkie a fix out of it, then sold the rest of the dope.

But Moon had been afraid to do business with the white boy. He wanted the business, so that only transactions had to go through King David, who was fronting for himself. Keeping the dope and selling it. Then when he planned to leave, he went to Moon and picked up five hundred dollars worth of dope, supposed to be going to the white boy who would then give the money to King David to pass on to Moon.

Moon was afraid to accept money from a peckerwood. That dope was what set King David up in Los Angeles. "China White" they called it when they had first seen the stuff from New York City.

"Hey, baby," King David yelled out to Jasper. "Come on and run down my tab, honey. I got big business to take care of."

Jasper came down the bar with her pad in her

hand, tearing off a sheet before she reached him. "There you go, big spender, twenty-six bucks." She flashed her best smile at him. You could never tell. Niggers like King David went to the top. He reminded her of a rat—sneaky, constantly plotting, trusting no human being.

King David dropped thirty dollars on the bar. "Keep the tip to buy you a dick, bitch," he said coldly as he turned his back on her.

Laughter from the people along the bar drowned out her reply. King walked briskly toward the door. He didn't want to really get her too mad, since he wasn't carrying his gun anymore. California had taught him enough about that unwanted police trouble. There was also the fact that New York gave you five flat years for possession. So if the crazy bitch got mad enough, he'd have to do some fast cutting, because he knew she had a razor.

If the barmaid's eyes could shoot darts, he'd have been stabbed to death before he reached the door. She was wishing him all the bad luck in the world.

The night was filled with a chilling breeze. King David put his head down and walked across the street swiftly. He opened the door on the white Eldorado and got in. The car was his castle, the first one he'd ever owned.

Still feeling the chill, he turned on the motor and pushed the heater up to eighty. Next, he played his favorite tape, Sarah Vaughan singing "Over the Rainbow." Ten minutes hadn't passed when a black Ford pulled up and parked behind his Caddie. Two men got out and quickly approached the car.

Seeing them coming, King David let his window down. Rockie and Alvin, Moon's two lieutenants, both approached on the driver's side. "What is it, brother?" King said loudly as the men came near. He fingered the magnum under the arm rest and felt assured. Since he didn't know either of the men, he'd have to wait until they committed themselves.

"King David?" It wasn't a question, it was just a way of letting the King know they knew him. Alvin, who had spoken his name, continued, "Moon says to tell you that it would be a hell of a lot better if you go uptown, away from him. You know, it just ain't big enough for two dogs, so don't get bit."

As the men spoke, King David didn't notice a green Chevy pull up and a young black girl get out. She stood beside the other car for a moment, then started walking toward them. King David removed an envelope from his pocket and held it out to the men.

"I hear Moon expects somethin'. You boys wouldn't happen to know how much it was?" David asked, holding the money out of reach.

"Let's not play games this late in the day, King. We came for a grand, cash money," Rockie stated, reaching for the envelope.

King gave it to him, glad to be rid of it, and them. "I guess that ends our little business, don't it?"

Neither man bothered to answer, nor to take the time to count the money. Rockie glanced into the envelope to make sure it was money. The small stack contained all one-hundred-dollar bills.

As King David started up his motor, he noticed a young attractive girl in a mini. The short skirt aroused him. Being a leg man he was interested. She was tall and lean, with well-shaped bow-legs. From what he could see, she seemed to be light brown.

Alvin went back and started up the Ford. He glanced over at Rockie. "It looks like Mike ain't bullshittin'. That's his young sister out there. Ain't never knowed him to bring her into anything."

Rockie shook his head in agreement. "Yeah, I wouldn't trade places with King David for all the tea in China." He glanced out the window as they drove past. They saw her motion for King David to join her.

King shook his head and waved to her to come over. "Come here, tender momma, it's chilly out there." He spoke loudly as he let the window down on the passenger side.

Before he finished speaking, she had started for the car. She walked with a proud step, knowing well that she was in her prime.

"What is it, honey?" she asked when she reached the car. She bent down and smiled, flashing well-kept, bright teeth.

She was younger than he had first thought. Now his interest was really aroused. He didn't believe she was over fifteen. What a beautiful mare this would be for a coming home present. Her skin looked so cool and golden brown that he wanted to reach out and touch it. As he stared at her, he mentally undressed her. Her young breasts would be straight out, without any sag. Firm and tender, something to stimulate a man like him.

"Come on and sit down, honey. It's kind of chilly out there," he said casually. He hit the door lock near his left hand.

She smiled at him, not bothering to open the door. "Let your window down, sweetie," she said in a light voice.

A frown crossed King David's face, but he decided to play it her way until he could talk her into the car. "What's wrong, sweet thing? You ain't changed your mind about a littl' bit of fun, have you?"

"What you talkin' 'bout, man? I ain't said nothin'. Just lookin', that's all." Her voice had a husky ring to it, revealing what was in store when she became mature.

Country girl, thought King David. All she wanted was to be begged, then she'd get in and end up fucking like a mule. King David thought he knew the type. Might be the first time she ever rode in a Cadillac. The longer he stared at the girl, though, the more he felt like he knew her. The face, there was something about it that he remembered. But it couldn't be. The kid wouldn't have been over ten when he left, and though he liked them young, he didn't mess with kids that young. It had to be a well-developed young girl to excite him.

The way she had of leaning back on her heels, her skirt tight against her legs, her head cocked to the side arrogantly. A light started blinking in his mind, and he knew he'd have his finger on it in a minute.

The voice reached him through the open window on the driver's side, which he hadn't bothered to roll back up, and took him completely by surprise. King David flinched. He prided himself on never losing his cool. But for a moment he did.

Twisting his neck around, King David saw the two of them, both holding pistols. Quickly, he tried to place them, but they were too young. Young jack-up artists, he thought instantly. If he didn't give them any trouble, they'd take the few hundred he had and leave happy.

"You must not be able to hear so good, punk. I said out!" It was the same voice, only this time King David really understood the words. He hated parting with his magnum, but it would have been useless to try removing the large pistol. He knew without a doubt that these men would kill him because if he got the chance he'd kill them.

As he opened the door, he glanced back at the young girl, but she was gone. It had been so fleeting it might as well have been a dream. To have been set up by a fifteen-year-old girl—a bitter smile curved at King David's lips. What a wonderful black-hearted bitch she would be for whoever controlled her.

"Move it, nigger!" the black man growled. For the first time King David took a good look at his jack-up artists. The eyes of the blacker one were dead and he didn't like the cold, fish-eyed nigger. But what he saw in the younger black's eyes shocked him. They were enraged. The boy's whole face showed that he was fighting for control. Tears were in the corners of his eyes. Whatever the reason, King David knew it would have gone better if he had tried to draw the heavy gun.

Even as the door closed, his agile mind told him that this was much more than a heist. For some reason, these men wanted to kill him. He had to find out why and talk. If they'd listen, he had a chance. Talking was his whole game. If somebody would listen, he had a story to tell.

Mike grabbed King David and shoved him toward the sidewalk. The little man was walking too slow. Mike came up on the sidewalk beside him and, instead of the gun, he now held a long switchblade.

People entering the bar noticed the small commotion, and now others looked out the window. "Well, I'll be damn, partner. We done collected an audience by accident," Blue told Mike quietly. "Don't look like you have much time, but if the nigger leaves here without knowing why, then the joke's on him." Suddenly the man's face seemed to come alive, and with it the dead fish eyes. They embodied something unspeakably evil and vile.

"Why, man, why?" King David screamed at the top of his voice as he stepped back and reached wildly for his knife. They meant to kill him, and he didn't want to die for no reason at all. "Take my money, man. Here!" He knew they didn't want his money, but he needed a second, and he got it.

Mike hesitated for a minute. He didn't want to kill him without letting him know why. He had lived this moment too many times. He wanted to see the little rat beg, then remind him of the young kid he had hit with the bottle.

Because of the moment's hesitation on Mike's part, Blue had to step around Mike. He knew the killing had to go off now; too many people were taking an interest in what was going on. Blue wished now that he had kept his gun in his hand. The knives had been Mike's idea, even though they used guns to force King David out of the car. With the long stiletto held firmly in his right hand, Blue moved around Mike quickly.

King David had two choices when he went to his coat pocket—to bring out his wallet or the long keen-bladed knife he kept next to his wallet. The money wouldn't do any good. He knew these men were going to cut them up a nigger. He couldn't understand why, but he thanked heaven that the boy had hesitated when he mentioned his money. He got his second and at least he'd have a chance to cut one of them; if the boy didn't move quick enough, he might get them both.

When Blue came in under King David's guard, he stabbed upward, starting from the stomach. Suddenly a pain exploded in the base of his neck.

King David screamed shrilly from the pain. He jerked back suddenly, breaking the blade off while part of it was still imbedded in him.

The action brought Mike out of his black thoughts, and he moved with swiftness. He struck and struck again. All the stab wounds were to the stomach. King David screamed from the pain, and the more he twisted away, the more the boy stalked him. He screamed from sheer pain now, and as he fell, Mike bent down and plunged the knife into his prone figure. Blood ran over Mike's hands, and his clothes were covered with it. He struck King David one more time, high in the chest.

"What the hell is going on?" It was a white voice, and that rang a bell instantly. Mike glanced up and saw a wildly bearded white man running toward them. He looked big enough to give them plenty of it, too. Mike turned and ran toward the waiting auto that was backing toward them down the street. Even as he ran toward the car, he saw Blue stumbling from one car to the other, holding himself up. He was hurt. Mike quickly caught up with him and helped him the rest of the way to the car.

"Goddamn," Mike's young sister Edna yelled at them. "Why didn't you just shoot the bastard and get it over with? Now look at the headache we got."

"Just shut up and drive, we ain't got no problems," Mike ordered sharply.

Paul Pawlowski leaned down over the neatly

dressed black man. The man gasped, "Mister, who-ever you are, don't let me die here in the streets. Please, mister," he begged, "I don't never want to die alone in the gutter."

Paul pulled the man's shirt back and knew at once that he couldn't live. Blood was bubbling out of the man's open chest. There was a gash from his lower stomach up to his chest. Paul could see the man's intestines seething beneath the shredded skin. The dying black man turned his head to the side and vomited blood and a sick-ening brown bile. Paul held his own stomach firm. He gently reached down and lifted the gored man up in his long arms and carried him up the steps toward his room.

Edna glanced at Blue's eye. She could see the metal blade protruding from it. Blood ran freely from the hole in the man's socket. It was a horri-ble wound and she twisted away from the sight.

"Are you mad?" Her voice began to rise. A chill-ing terror invaded her. The thought of Blue lying beside her bleeding, hurt so bad that he needed immediate help from a doctor frightened her. "We ain't got no problems?" She screamed the words back at Mike.

In her blind, growing rage at her brother, Edna momentarily lost control of the steering wheel and sideswiped a parked car.

"Goddamn it," Mike roared, "drive the car and let me worry about Blue!" The order was sharp, harsh enough to make her concentrate on her driving.

Mike glanced back over his shoulder at the rear window. Goddamn it! The curse word roared over and over in his mind. He had gotten the dirty motherfucker after all the waiting. His life was complete. The only dream he had ever had was of killing King David. Now it was over. His mind refused to face the reality of their next step.

5

PAUL PAWLOWSKI LEANED down beside the well-dressed black man. Blood was seeping through the man's light dress shirt. As Paul's face drew near, the man gasped.

"Help me to my car, mister. Don't want to die layin' in no gutter." King David gripped Paul's arm firmly. "I'll pay you, mister. Don't mind payin', just don't want to die alone in the street."

Paul pulled back the shirt and examined the wounds. Instantly he knew the man at his feet had spoken the truth. He was going to die. The wound in his chest alone had been enough to kill him. Paul glanced down at the hand on his arm. It was bloody. When Paul pried the fingers loose, there was a ring of blood around his sleeve.

"My car's at the curb. Help me, friend." King could feel his strength leaving. "Please, mister?" he begged. He had seen too many black men bleed their life's blood out on the dirty floor of a pool-room, or inside some dimly lit nightclub.

Paul glanced over at the expensive car near the curb. What the hell, he told himself. If the guy wanted to die in his own car, at least he could help the poor bastard die where he chose. Slowly and with care, Paul lifted the man.

The man in his arms made a deep moan as Paul steadied himself with the load. He made his way slowly toward the car. He was careful as he placed the man down inside the automobile. Paul ran around the car and jumped in behind the steering wheel. He doubted whether his patient would hold up that long, but since they were in the car, they might as well rush over to the nearest hospital.

Paul didn't have to search for the keys; they were already in the car. He started the motor. The sound of the wounded man's voice came to him clearly.

"Ain't no use, man. I done cashed in the big ticket." King David's voice got weaker as he continued. "Life's a bitch, man. It just ain't no win. Here I thought I had Jesus in a jug, no lookin' back. Done stung for all the bread a nigger needs to get over with, now this shit come up out of nowhere. Can you dig it?" He tried to laugh, but blood rushing out of his mouth choked him.

"Just take it easy, fellow," Paul said as he expertly drove the big car in and out of the light evening traffic. "It won't be long before I have you at the hospital, then everything will be all right."

This time King David did manage to laugh. "Big fuckin' deal, man," he answered dryly. "It wouldn't make any difference if we were at two hospitals right now. Ain't nothing a doctor can do for me now, man. I done bought the big ticket; it ain't but one more step left for me." The wounded man fell silent; his last words seemed to linger in the air.

Paul tried to change the mood. "I don't know about that, buddy; you can never tell. I glanced at your wounds and I've seen guys live with worse ones." Paul knew that the wounded man knew that he was lying.

"Okay, brother," King David stated, "have it your way. I just don't want to die alone, that's all. Just picturing myself stretched out in that fuckin' street dying alone is damn near too much to bear."

"Don't think about it!" Paul cautioned sharply. "Think about gettin' patched up. Why don't you try to save some of your strength? Don't talk so much; you ain't doing nothing but wearing yourself out."

As the car went over a slight bump in the street, King David let out a grunt. His face twisted up hideously from the pain. "Talkin' helps to take my fuckin' mind off the pain, man. It's all I got left. Life is a motherfuckin' bitch," he stated again, this time more bitterly than before. "It's not fair. I mean, a guy busts his ass trying to reach up and pull himself out of the fuckin' gutters, then when he can finally see some kind of light, some shit like this happens. Oh no, baby, it just ain't right. It couldn't happen to nobody else but me." Tears

rolled down the man's cheeks as he talked. "All I been through, everything I've done, I mean, ain't no way it should end like this."

"This ain't got to be the end," Paul stated feebly. He realized that he was just using words, saying anything to fill the void.

King David continued as if Paul hadn't spoken. "I've always tried to be honest with myself, but now, when I'm face to face with the final act, I can't accept it. Not this." He broke down and began to sob. Deep sobs, the kind that no one should ever witness of another.

Paul glanced at the man out of the corner of his eyes. Damn! he cursed. It looked like King David had taken a bath in blood. His suit coat was completely covered from where it had seeped through his shredded shirt. Even the upholstery in the car was covered with the dark reddish stain of blood. Where King David's arm rested on the front seat, a small pool of blood had formed.

Christ almighty, Paul swore, how much blood can this guy lose without passing out? If he doesn't die from the stab wounds, the poor bastard should bleed to death before we get to the hospital. As he took another quick look at the wounded man, Paul thought that the injured man had finally passed away.

King David's head had dropped onto his chest and it appeared as if he had stopped breathing. But it was not death that closed the man's mouth.

The pain had finally reached unbearable stages. King David closed his eyes and gritted his teeth. He tried to slump back against the door padding. Maybe if he lay in another position it would ease some of the hurt. He tried to breathe lightly but every time he took any kind of deep breath, he could feel the pain all over his chest.

"This dying crap is one hell of a job," King David managed to say. Somehow talking seemed to relieve the pain.

Paul stared over at the man in astonishment. He was surprised that the man was still alive and noticed that the man's voice was growing much weaker. It wouldn't be long now, he reflected.

"Just hold on a little longer," Paul stated as he pressed down harder on the gas pedal. "The hospital's just a couple of blocks away." When they had first got in the car, he wouldn't have taken odds that the man would live to reach the hospital. He had just been going through the motions.

"You know, if it hadn't been for you, mister, I'd still be laying back there in the street."

"It wasn't nothin' anybody else wouldn't do. I just happened to be the one that came along at the time, that's all," Paul stated.

King David didn't waste his strength answering, but both men knew that the statement was a lie. He would have lain in the gutter until the police arrived, then they would have left him there while they called for an ambulance. No way in the world would they have put him in the police car bleeding the way he was bleeding. He would have lain there and died in the gutter, the thing he had always feared. Paul had been the one person in a hundred, a man who didn't mind getting involved. King David knew that a black man wouldn't have taken the chance. The average black man would have crossed the street and hurried on his way before he'd allow himself to get involved in a murder.

For one of the few times in his life King David felt gratitude. It was a strange feeling for him. He was a man used to playing on people who were unlucky enough to cross his path. He took kindness for weakness, friendship as an opportunity to take advantage of the person foolish enough to offer it. The pain in his body was everywhere. Never before had he hurt like he was hurting now. The sight of the hospital gave him a sense of relief. He tried to blank out the pain as they entered the lane that led to the emergency entrance.

The emergency ward was at the rear of the hospital. Paul drove the car down to the back doors and parked next to an ambulance. As he got out and ran around the car, he waved to an attendant standing on the back dock taking a smoke.

"Hey, buddy, how about giving me a hand here. I've got a man who's hurt real bad." Paul opened the door on the passenger side.

The short Negro on the dock came down the ramp pushing a wheelchair. The man let out a whistle when he saw all the blood on King David. "Looks like somebody been butcherin' steers in-

side that car," he said as he maneuvered the wheelchair in place.

Paul didn't bother to answer the man as he
reached in and grabbed King David under the
armpits. Both men tried to lift him as gently as
possible, but a cry of pain escaped from the
wounded man as they lifted him from the car.
When they set him down in the wheelchair, his
head dropped down over his chest. As Paul straightened up from placing King David's feet together
on the wheelchair foot-rest, he looked at the head
resting lifelessly on his chest. At once Paul believed the man had finally died.

"Looks like he didn't make it to the hospital
after all," Paul said quietly.

"He ain't dead!" The orderly stated flatly as he
began to push the chair toward the ramp. "You
better park your car back out of the way, then
come on in. I'll take him on ahead and get some
doctors to start work on him as soon as possible."
Without another word, the man rushed on up the
ramp, pushing the wheelchair as fast as he could.

Paul glanced around quickly, trying to spot
somewhere to park the car. He got in and drove
slowly back around to the visitors' parking lot.
For a minute he was undecided on what to do. It
would be easier just to leave the car and go on
about his business. That way, he wouldn't become
any more involved than he was already. After all,
he had done all that he could do. It didn't make
sense to get any more involved. But someone

should know where the man's car was, he reasoned. After parking, he walked slowly toward the entrance of the hospital.

As soon as he entered, the short black orderly rushed up to him. "What's your name, mate?" the man asked quickly.

Paul hesitated, then gave it to him. He watched the man hurry off toward the rear of the hospital. As he stood in the hallway, an officer walked up to him. "You're the guy who brought the Negro in who was all cut up, aren't you?" the white policeman inquired in a harsh voice.

For a minute Paul didn't want to answer, but finally he shook his head in agreement. "Yeah, I saw him in front of the building where I live and rushed him down here."

The policeman removed a pencil from his pocket. "Well, I'm going to have to make a report on it, so you might as well relax. You and I are going to be here together for a few minutes."

Paul let out a sigh. "I knew it was coming," he said quietly. "Before this shit stops, I'm going to wish that I had never gotten involved."

The tall, red-faced officer grinned, revealing yellow teeth. "Yeah, well, it's too late to cry over spilled milk now. If you didn't want to get involved, you should have left the nigger laying in the street."

Paul glanced up at the man. "Would you have left him lying in the street?" he asked and knew the answer at once.

"Well, I'll tell you this much," the officer began,

"I wouldn't have gotten his blood all over my clothes." For the first time, Paul glanced down and saw the front of his only suit covered with dark spots of blood.

The sight of the blood on his clothes didn't anger him half as much as the officer's attitude. He tried to conceal his anger, but it was difficult to keep it out of his voice. "Okay, so I got a little blood on my clothes. You think that's more important than trying to save a guy's life?"

The white officer laughed. "If the shoe had been on the other foot, you think that guy back there would have gone through the trouble of gettin' his clothes bloody while rushing you to the hospital? You can bet your ass he wouldn't have bothered. If anything, he'd have been busy trying to beat you out of your wallet."

Before Paul could give his angry reply, the orderly rushed up. In his hands he was holding an envelope. "Hey mate, you done hit a gold mine."

Paul glanced around at him, not understanding what the man was saying. "How's the guy I brought in?"

The orderly shook his head. "He passed away, buddy. There was nothing the doctors could do for him. He had been cut too many times. I'm surprised he lived as long as he did."

The white officer and Paul stared at each other. The thought of the man dying left an empty feeling inside Paul. He hadn't known the man, but he had hoped, even though his common sense told him the man couldn't live, that by some luck he might pull through. It hadn't happened, and now it was all for nothing. But not really, Paul remembered. The man hadn't wanted to die in the gutter, so Paul had saved him from that fate.

The orderly held out the envelope. "Here, mate, the guy made you his beneficiary; that's why I needed your name. He had the doctors as witnesses and left you everything, even the problem of buryin' him."

At once, before the orderly could say any more, the policeman burst out laughing. Paul looked at him angrily. But the orderly was serious. His eyes were cold and angry. "It ain't no welfare case, mate; he left you enough money to bury him with." The orderly glared around at the officer. "Yeah, mate, from what I witnessed, I'd say you came out of the deal damn well. The poor guy knew he couldn't live, so he spent the last few minutes of his time tryin' to repay you for the trouble you went through. In this envelope is some cash money, plus the pink to his car. He signed it over to you. Seems as if it's paid for. He had the doctors witness everything he did. He also said to tell you that he had some notes he'd written down about himself, and that he hoped you wouldn't destroy them without reading some of it." The orderly handed Paul the envelope. "You'll find enough money inside to bury him properly if you should decide to follow his wishes."

"Hey, wait a minute there," the policeman said, "I don't know if this is right or not. You had better give that envelope to me. After I check it out with my office, then I'll let you know if it's all right or not."

Before the officer could reach out and take it, the orderly yanked it back. "Maybe you didn't hear what I said, officer. I said the man had the doctors sign as witnesses, so you don't have a damn thing to do with what's in this envelope. The man left it to this guy. It was his last request. He did it so that he wouldn't have to be buried by the city, and here you are trying to spoil it all. No way, I mean it. If I were to give this to you, it would be tied up downtown until after this man is buried, and his last wish would be spoiled. Now you haven't any right whatsoever to his belongings. They go to his nearest kin, or wife, or whatever, and since the man had three doctors sign a note to the effect that he was in his right mind, you are way out of line trying to take his last request from him."

The orderly turned to Paul. "Nobody can force you to spend the money he left you to bury him, but I do hope you will see to it that he doesn't have to be buried by the city. He asked me to tell you this."

Paul shook his head dumbfoundedly. Things were happening too damn fast for him to really know what was up or down. "If he left enough money to buy a casket, I'll get it for him, and if it's not enough, I'll sell the car and raise the money. I give you my word on it," Paul said and took the envelope from the orderly. As he walked toward the front entrance of the hospital the orderly relaxed. For some reason he believed the tall young white man would keep his word.

Paul didn't open the envelope until he got home. He waited until he had boiled some coffee and sat down on the edge of the bed. The first thing that fell out was a diamond-studded watch. A large diamond ring came next. Paul smiled. Here were two articles that he wouldn't have bought himself. He would feel funny if he sold them, so he tried the ring on. It fit tightly on the small finger of his right hand. He slipped the expensive watch on and smiled as he watched the diamonds glitter.

Suddenly the sound of loud music came from downstairs. He knew that the simple-minded girl who worked as a waitress somewhere had finally come home. At times she would play her record player all night long, as loud as the cheap machine would go.

Once he had been foolish enough to go downstairs and ask her kindly if she would please turn it down. But that had angered her, and for the next five nights she had kept it on all night long just for spite. Now he knew better. Either he stuck cotton in his ears or he pulled out his typewriter and tried to write until she tired of the music. It was so loud that there was no possible way in the world for him to go to sleep as long as she kept it on.

Next to come out of the envelope was King David's wallet. The sight of the money crammed inside the wallet caused Paul to gasp. He removed the money and began counting slowly. When he finished, he counted it again to make sure he hadn't made any mistake. There was close to two thousand dollars. Paul put the money back and sat quietly on the edge of the bed. There was one thing he was sure of now. He would be able to give the dead man a good burial.

The sound of the loud music began to get on his nerves, so he got up and went out to the car. He opened the trunk, thinking about the notebook that was inside the trunk somewhere. He saw a small overnight bag and removed it. Next he took out an expensive black suitcase and its matching mate. Paul made his way back upstairs and pushed open the door to his small flat. The sound of the music could still be heard, but now that he had something else on his mind, it didn't disturb him half as much as it had earlier. The first thing Paul opened was the overnight bag. He fumbled around inside it until he found a black diary that would have fit well with some woman's belongings.

With patience, he opened the diary and glanced at the first page. He smiled as he read the introduction: "The life story of a born player." With this beginning, Paul made himself more comfortable and began to read.

6

AS EDNA DROVE UP and down the streets it became clear to her that her brother Mike didn't
know what to do. She knew that they couldn't
just keep driving around aimlessly.

"Mike," she said, "we are going to have to do
something. Blue done passed out, and if he don't
get to a doc soon, we goin' have a dead man on
our hands."

Her words fell on deaf ears. Mike was too busy
remembering the joy he felt when he stuck the
knife into King David. When Edna slammed on
her brakes and parked the car, he came to his
senses.

"I'm not going any farther," she stated harshly.
"I went along with you when you asked me to
drive while you took care of King David 'cause of
what he did to Mother, but I ain't going along
with this stupid-ass driving around, 'cause it don't

make sense. Now you tell me what we goin' do
about Blue. He is supposed to be your friend, so
it would seem as if you would be concerned
about what happened to him."

"Okay, okay," Mike roared. "I said I'd take care
of everything, so what's the problem? Find me a
pay phone; I'll call Moon."

She laughed, and with that laugh the sting of
her words were not too vicious. "Moon! Yeah,
Mike, let's hurry up and call the great godfather.
He'll take care of all our problems."

Mike glanced over at his sister sharply. He had
never been able to figure out why she disliked
Moon so much. The man had never done anything
to her to his knowledge. But for some reason,
whenever Moon's name was brought in, she became sarcastic.

Even though she had spoken that way about
Moon, Edna started the motor up without another word and drove off. She didn't have to go
far before she found a pay telephone. She parked
in front of it and cut the motor.

As Mike jumped out, Blue let out a loud moan.
His head fell over on the seat at an angle. Blood
and pus ran out of the open wound. Edna turned
her head away. If they didn't find help quick, Blue
would be a dead man. That was one thing she was
sure of.

For the thousandth time, she cursed herself for
being foolish enough to get involved with her
brother in his stupid revenge. She had forgotten
about King David years ago. What had happened

66

should have been left alone. It had been their mother's fault for getting involved with a man like King David.

Some traffic came past their parked car and she scanned the automobiles closely, hoping that their luck would hold and a police car wouldn't cruise by. Edna was positive that someone had called in and given the description of their car to the police after she had sideswiped those other cars. Just the thought of her silly driving made her blush with shame.

Edna considered herself an expert driver, so it was a blow to her pride that in her panic she had driven so badly when she should have been at her best. She had always prided herself on her control whenever things got bad. To be coolheaded in the clutches was something to be proud of.

On the second ring, a man answered the telephone. Mike quickly asked for Moon after giving his name. In a matter of seconds Moon was on the other telephone. Moon's voice was soft and full of confidence as he spoke.

"Hey, Mike, how's tricks, my man?" Moon asked lightly. From his voice it wasn't possible for the man on the other end of the line to know that Moon had been pacing the floor in a rage only moments before. He had gotten the news earlier about the hit on King David. He had even called the hospitals until he found which one the white man had taken King David to. He knew King David was dead. He also knew that the license number of the car Mike and Blue had used had been given to the police by an informer who had witnessed the whole thing from a window of the bar.

What put oil on the fire and put Moon in a rage was that people always talked about things they didn't know about and came up with wrong answers. The wrong answer that was bothering him was the fact that too many people knew Moon was supposed to have met King David, so they would figure Moon was responsible for the hit. Once it came out that Mike and Blue were responsible for the hit, nobody would believe that Moon didn't have anything to do with it. No matter how much he swore his innocence, people would still hold him to blame.

And that wasn't the worst part of it. If Blue or Mike got busted, they could make a deal with the police just by mentioning Moon's name. The police would promise them all kinds of deals if they'd just involve the big man. While all this was on Moon's mind, he never let a hint of it out to Mike.

"Yeah, Mike, what can I do for you, guy?" Moon inquired easily.

"Hey Moon, I need your help, man. I know you told me I was on my own, but we run into trouble," Mike said quickly.

"Yeah, brother, you know you can depend on old Moon. What's the deal?"

"We run into a little trouble, Moon. Blue fucked around and got careless and got stabbed. He got stabbed in the eye, man, I don't know if he goin' make it or not." Mike spoke quickly, then continued when there was no comment from the other end of the line. "He needs a doctor bad, Moon. I mean he needs one real bad."

I wish the sonofabitch was dead, Moon thought coldly as he listened, but when he spoke, his words and voice didn't reveal his inner thoughts. "Okay, Mike, don't worry. Them things happen, baby, so just keep your cool."

"I knew you wouldn't let me down, Moon, I just knew it, boss."

"I don't never let down none of my boys, Mike, and you know you're one of my favorite men, so don't worry. Old man Moon will take care of everything for you. Now listen, you must still be in the same car, right?" Moon didn't wait for an answer. "And Blue's too hurt to leave the ride and walk or catch a cab, so you goin' have to take a chance on driving the car you're in."

"I don't think our ride is hot, Moon," Mike replied.

You wouldn't, you stupid bastard, Moon reflected as he listened to Mike before cutting the flow of words off. "Listen, Mike. Okay, maybe the car ain't hot, but just in case, where the hell are you?"

He waited until Mike gave him their location. "Okay, fine, there's a parkin' garage on 110th Street, just about four blocks from where you're at right now. So you and Blue get the hell over there and pull inside the garage and park in the back of the goddamn garage, you got that? In the rear of the joint, okay? I'm going to send some boys down there in another car to pick you guys

NEVER DIE ALONE

up and get Blue over to a doctor I know. Now just be careful, Mike, and everything will work out all right. Oh yeah, did you pick up my money?"

Mike felt his breast pocket. "Yeah, Moon, you know I take care of business. I got it right here in my pocket, don't worry about a thing."

Don't worry, huh, you stupid sonofabitch, Moon cursed to himself. "Okay then, we ain't got no problems. You just do like I said. Take it easy and drive slow. The boys will be right there, so don't get nervous."

"Hey Moon," Mike yelled before Moon could hang up, "say, man, I got my kid sister with me. You think I better drop her off first before I get to the garage?"

For the first time Moon blew his cool. "Hell no," he cursed loudly, "you don't do no dumb-ass thing like that! The only fuckin' chance you got right now is havin' the broad along. If some cop car should ride past and see her in the car, they might not harass you, but just you and Blue alone? Shit, man, think it out for yourself. You say Blue's hurt, didn't you?"

Moon wiped the sweat off his brow, then picked a pencil off the bar and began to write out an address as he continued to talk. "You keep her with you, Mike. I'll have another guy come along just to drop her off, but she stays with you until the boys get there. You can even fake the people out in the garage by sittin' in the car with a broad along. But two men, it makes people suspicious."

"Yeah, I see what you mean, Moon," Mike replied quickly as he glanced out the pay booth at Edna in the car. He could see Blue lying out on the car seat. Even from where he was, Blue didn't look good.

"Okay, then we done wasted enough time rappin', man. Let's get down to business," Moon ordered, then hung up. He turned on the four men standing around watching them. "Well now," he began, "that was the fool there. He's in trouble, and Blue's been hurt."

Moon walked around his bar and pushed a button. A panel with glasses on a small ledge began to slide backwards. When it was open, a man sitting on one of the expensive bar stools could see the various weapons hanging from the pegs inside the compartment. Moon reached in and removed two sawed-off shotguns and placed them on the bar. He then placed two pistols next to the shotguns.

"Now I want all four of you guys to go along on this deal, so that nothing can go wrong. Park in the rear of the garage; I'll have called and made arrangements so that the back door will be open. Park your cars back there. You had better take two of them along so that, if anything goes wrong, you'll have another way of gettin' clear. But shouldn't nothing go wrong on this deal. Blue is already hurt, so he won't be no problem, and Mike won't be expectin' nothing either, so he won't be no trouble. The broad has got to be knocked off along with them. Mike has some cash on him, a grand, and you boys can keep it. When you guys get back, there will be four thousand more waitin' on you." Again Moon wiped the sweat off his brow. "That's all I can tell you, except be damn sure you kill every fuckin' one of them!"

Moon picked up one of the shotguns and held it out to a tall baldheaded black man. "Earl, I want you to be in charge of this littl' detail, so I'm givin' you one of the shatter guns. You can give the other one to whoever you think will handle it right. I just don't want no slip-ups."

The slim dark Negro handled the gun smoothly. It seemed to be part of him once he took it into his hands. "Don't worry about a thing, Moon. I don't like workin' with this many people, but for you anything goes."

He tossed the other shotgun to a short light-skinned man with bad skin. "Here, Red, I trust you enough not to trust you, so you're my best bet." He grinned at Moon. "Red likes the sight of blood, so he's the ideal man for using one of these here little gems."

Earl laughed loudly at his so-called joke, then started for the door. He didn't bother to look back. The other two men removed the pistols from the barstool and quickly followed the first pair out of the apartment.

As soon as he finished talking on the telephone, Mike hurried back to the car. When he opened the door, Blue slumped over on his side. Mike had to lift the unconscious man back up before he could sit down. He stared at the broken blade imbedded in Blue's eyeball. The sight of it was almost enough to make a man vomit.

Edna saw the expression on his face. "It sure is a bad-lookin' wound, ain't it, Mike?" She started the motor. "Well," she asked, "what did big brother say? Is he coming to our rescue?"

"Yeah! He gave me an address to go to. He's going to have some people pick Blue up and take him over to a doc that they use for things like this," Mike stated importantly. "I been tellin' you, sis, that Moon looks out for the people who work for him. I mean, this ain't no short stoppin' organization that Moon runs, Edna. He's big-time."

"Yeah, yeah, I know," she replied quietly, relieved that the responsibility of taking care of Blue would drop on somebody else's shoulders instead of theirs.

She took another long look at Blue, and again the thought entered her mind that he was hurt a lot worse than they imagined him to be. He seemed to have gone into a coma. The way the man moaned and groaned while unconscious revealed to some extent just how serious the man's injury was. Edna had her doubts about whether or not a doctor could help Blue out now. There was one thing she was sure of: he'd never see out of the injured eye again. She'd bet money on that.

"Take your time, sis. We ain't got to go but over to 110th Street, so ain't no reason to speed," Mike stated nervously as he took a quick look over his shoulder.

The sound of a police siren in the distance caused both of them to become frightened. Edna started to park the car but Mike ordered her to keep on driving.

"It ain't for us, girl; just keep your cool," Mike cautioned, trying to appear more assured than he actually was.

"We just done come so close to being at an end to this shit, Mike, I'd hate for something to happen now," Edna said as she drove slowly onward.

Both of them counted the blocks slowly as they went by. "Just one more to go," Edna said, speeding up.

"Yeah, baby, at the next corner turn right. The garage is on the left-hand side of the street. But slow this goddamn car down, girl. We don't want to get stopped now," he yelled loudly.

For a moment Blue mumbled something, but neither one of the occupants in the car could understand what he had said.

"Just hold on, Blue, just hold on, partner," Mike stated, as he leaned down and spoke softly in Blue's ear, as if that would make the man understand him better.

The only reaction from Blue was a loud groan. Mike sat up straight, wondering for the first time whether or not his friend was going to make it. It was obvious that Blue was in bad shape.

"I don't know, Edna," Mike began, "I ain't never seen nobody hurt like this before. I mean, I saw guys cut up but never stabbed in the eye. Damn, it sure as hell looks bad, don't it?"

Edna waited until she made the right-hand turn before answering. "Shit, Mike, I don't even believe a doctor is going to be able to help him. I know he ain't goin' never be able to use that eye again," she stated as she slowed down and started to watch for the garage.

"There it is, sis, on the right-hand side of the street. Just pull right up to the door. Somebody will open it from the inside."

She followed his orders and pulled up into the driveway. Before they had reached the door, it began to go up. Edna slowly drove inside as the door started to come back down.

"Just keep on toward the back," Mike ordered. The man who had opened the door waved them on, standing in the doorway of a small office. As the car went past, he sat back down and made a move on the checkerboard that was on the desk. The other elderly man in the office had remained seated in an old wooden chair. He grinned as he moved his hand and picked up a checker and made a jump.

"Maybe if you had some more customers you'd make some more dumb moves like that," the old man said as he continued jumping until he had taken three pieces.

"Yeah," his friend replied, his mind drifting away from the simple game they were playing. "Maybe that's just what I need."

As he spoke two cars pulled up in the alleyway. Earl, in the first car, waved Red, the driver of the second car, past. He searched for a good parking place and found one. He had been looking for someplace where he wouldn't be blocked in.

"Well, Duke," Earl said to the man next to him, "we might as well get the ball rolling."

"Ain't no time like the present, Earl," Duke answered, opening the car door and climbing out.

Both men walked side by side until they reached the second car.

As Red and his partner Charles got out, Earl spoke directly to Red. "I'm wonderin' if we might not be better off to leave somebody with the machines to make sure don't nobody double park and block one of us in. What do you think about it?"

"You might be right, Earl," Red replied quickly. "We don't really need no four men for this shit, so maybe if we left Charles behind, it would make things go a hell of a lot better when it came time to get the hell away. I done seen more than one motherfucker get wasted 'cause his ride couldn't be used when he needed it."

"Yeah," Earl said quickly, "I think we better." He turned to the man with Red. "Charles, you get the easy part this time, my man. Just make sure you don't let no punks block either one of the rides in. I guess you can handle that without no problem, can't you?" He didn't wait for the man to answer. Earl started walking on down the alley that led to the garage. He felt the sawed-off shotgun under his suit coat, making sure it was in place.

When he reached the door of the garage he stopped and glanced back at the two men with him. "Okay," he said slowly, "this is the way we play it. We don't go in with guns out. We go in and check everything out. Mike don't suspect nothing, so we ain't got no problem. You, Duke, you take care of Blue. Red, you knock the cunt off, and I handle Mike. Now everybody knows who he's supposed to hit, so it won't be no fuck-up, with everybody shootin' wildly at whoever he sees. This way, each one of us has a fuckin' target. Be sure to put at least two good slugs into your goddamn target, 'cause Moon don't want no motherfuckin' mix-up on this one!"

Earl waited until both men had nodded their heads in agreement, then pushed open the back door of the garage.

7

AFTER PAUL GOT his coffee, he sat back on the bed and made himself comfortable as he opened the diary again. He noticed at once that it had been written in the first person. But after that, he forgot to read it with a critical eye for grammar or spelling, because he became too interested in what he read.

My plans have been made, so today should be my last day in New York. If everything goes right, I should be on my way out on the evening flight to California. The only reason I'm delaying my departure is that today is Mother's Day, and I have two women who receive checks. There is also the chance of me rippin' off Moon for a nice piece of heroin, and it's too good a chance to pass up. For the past two months I've been settin' Moon up for just this day, so it's been well planned.

Well, things have went just fine so far. I met Moon up on 127th Street and got two pieces of dope from him. He expects the money later on in the day after I collect from the women he thinks I have in my make-believe stable. It took a while to get him to the point where he would trust me with so much dope, but since he knows I don't use, he isn't worried. Far be it, his pride is so big that he doesn't think a nigger would have the nerve to bum him, the dumb-ass fool!

Yes, I wouldn't rip him off if I was planning on staying here, because I know his anger would be out of sight, but Moon ain't nothing but a Harlem hoodlum who would never have the resources to reach as far as the West Coast for someone who has ripped him off. Now that I've got the dope, all that's holding me back now is the mailman. I'm going over to Vera's house now and get her check. After I promise to bring her a piece of dope back for it, she won't be any trouble either.

Well, that didn't take long. I wasn't gone but an hour. The stupid bitch was waiting for me with the check. After taking her to get it cashed, I left her sitting in a restaurant with the promise that I would be back at her apartment in about an hour. As I write this shit, I wonder if anybody would ever read it and believe that people could be so dumb. Since this morning I've collected three pieces of heroin and a check for two hundred and twenty dollars.

Vera has six kids and I do wonder how the dumb bitch is going to make it without some kind of money. I was even tempted to leave her with ten or twenty dollars, something she could have used to buy some food for the kids. But on second thought, I realized that, if I had left her with twenty dollars, she wouldn't have bought food for her kids, hell no. The bitch would have bought some dope to take care of that monkey she got on her back.

So that is one damn monkey that's going to go hungry for a few days, or hours. No tellin', a junkie-ass bitch can get money where the average person wouldn't be able to raise a cent, so I'm not too worried about her.

Goddamn, but did I have trouble collecting that check from Edna. She didn't want to give me none of it. Told me she had to buy clothes for her children and some other bullshit. Had to kick the shit out of her, plus hit that punk-ass son of hers with a bottle. What was his name? Mike, I think, yeah, that's it. Had to knock two of his front teeth out with a Coke bottle before I could get out of their flat with the money.

The old bitch fought like hell for her few
dollars, even though she's been givin' me
part of her check for the past three months.
Well, that just goes to show you can never figure a cunt out. Here she was the only one I
figured I wouldn't have any trouble with.
Just promise her I'd bring her the money
back in a day or two, but she wouldn't buy
no part of it.

Sorry about the trouble but I'm not takin'
any chances. Leavin' for the airport right
now. You can never tell, the bitch might
even go to the police. That's all I need right
now, a fuckin' case with the police. If things
go well, my next entry in this diary will be
from California.

Paul laid the diary down and took a sip from
his coffee. He shook his head in wonderment.
The sounds coming from the downstairs apartment didn't even disturb him as he picked up the
diary and continued to read.

Arrived in California at eleven o'clock at
night. Didn't know a person in Los Angeles
so I just told the cab driver at the airport to
take me to a good motel in Hollywood. He
dropped me in front of the Golden Eagle
Motel on Wilcox Avenue. After checking in, I
counted my bankroll. I had over seven hundred dollars in my raise, so I didn't have to
worry about the rent for a while.

Paul read the next page in surprise, then set the diary down. He stared at the wall for a second, then reread the next page again. "That's it!" he exclaimed, his voice sounding loud in the empty apartment. The poor sonofabitch was really trying to write a book! Now I wonder just how much of this shit in here is real and how much is just an overworked imagination. Paul studied the handwriting before him. Maybe the guy was really planning on trying to sell this shit to some publisher, Paul reflected.

As his coffee began to cool, Paul drained the last of it from his cup. He picked the diary up and continued from where he had left off. He grinned to himself as he began to read dialogue. Now that King David's diary began to have an exchange of conversation between different people, Paul was sure that King David was either writing his autobiography or had written a pretty good beginning for a work of fiction.

The motel room was hip. Wall-to-wall carpet, plus a color television with a waterbed. Being on the safe side, I stashed the heroin inside a pair of shorts, then put them in the compartment where I kept my dirty clothes. This was in case I happened to get a snoopy maid or one that stole. In any case, I didn't think she'd bother to look inside my dirty laundry bag.

Damn! Been laying out in a lawn chair near the pool. This is something a poor black-ass

nigger like me ain't used to. And the friend-
liness of these white chicks out here in unbelievable. If the studs back in the Big Apple
only knew how friendly these white broads
are out here, it would be a black tidal wave
'cause of so many black motherfuckers leaving and heading for the sunny shores of Los
Angeles. Got to get dressed now. I made a
date with a cute blonde I met at the pool.
Dinner, then a few drinks at some club she
says is mellow.

Janet took me to Club 21 near Hollywood
and Vine. The inside of the nightclub was
something out of a movie. I mean it's goin'
take some gettin' used to after them crummy
joints I been used to hangin' out in back
home. Janet is something to write home
about herself. Blonde, with a shape like a brick
shit-house. I ain't never spoke to a white girl
that looks this good before, let alone took
one out.

I think I could have laid the bitch after we
got back from clubbin', but I didn't want to
rush things or give her the idea that the only
thing I wanted from her was a piece of ass.
Also found out her weakness. The fine-ass
bitch likes coke. Well, if she likes cocaine I
think I got just the thing for her. She also
hinted that most of the crowd she ran around
with snorted cocaine. If that's the case, this
will be just the break I need to get rid of the
heroin I got.

I don't think none of the peckerwoods know the difference between girl or boy, so I'm going to sell them heroin for cocaine if it looks right. The first time I get a chance, I think I'll slip her some boy and see if she knows the difference. If she doesn't—baby baby baby—it will be smooth sailing for me!

Ain't got but a minute, so I'll just jot this down. Janet is takin' me shoppin' so that I can pick up a bathing suit. Can you dig my black ass, a country boy, layin' out next to the swimming pool beside all that fine white trim? It's hard to believe, but it's true. Got to go; she just called.

Paul grinned as he professionally noticed when the diary stopped being a diary and became a novel. King David must have been a lonely man, Paul reasoned as he read on.

"Hi, Janet. Damn girl, you're even more lovely than what you were last night, if that's possible."

She laughed brightly as she stepped into my apartment. Before closing the door, I glanced out to see who had seen her come into my motel room. I noticed three women at the pool glancing toward my door, so I knew she hadn't entered without being noticed.

"Hi, David. Are you ready to go on our little shopping spree?" Her voice was more

husky when she spoke than I had remembered.

"In just a minute, Janet," I answered, as I
tried not to stare at her. But it was impossible not to look at the tall, narrow-featured
blonde. Her hair was straight, like most white
girls wore their hair nowadays, hanging down
on her shoulders. Every now and then she'd
toss her head back to get the hair out of her
face, then you could see her eyes. Her eyes
were something else just by themselves. Or
maybe it was just me since I'd never had a
blue-eyed woman before. I was fascinated
by them.

"Well, honey," she said, snapping me out
of the trance I had fallen into, "don't you remember me? I'm the same person you brought
home at four o'clock this mornin' and left so
rudely at my door." She smiled at me when
she said this, kidding me about being so
proper. Because, as I mentioned, I didn't try
and get into her pants last night or this morning, I just took her to her door and then
walked around the pool and entered my own
room.

I grinned back at her. This broad didn't
believe in bullshittin'. She came right out
with it. I decided to check out my thoughts
on the cocaine. "Hey, Janet, don't come down
on me so hard, please. I was just wonderin'
should I offer you a snort of this coke I got

or should I wait until after we come back from shoppin'?"

"If you know what's good for you, you had better wait until after we get our shopping done or there won't be any shopping trip this day. Once I get some of that cocaine up my big nose," she stated in her husky voice, then rolled her eyes toward the bed, "well, David, I don't think I'm going to have to spell it out for you, am I?"

We both laughed at that. She looked so serious when she rolled her eyes toward the bed that I couldn't help but take her in my arms. We kissed slowly at first, then as I felt her fingers moving up and down my back I crushed her in my arms. I could feel her legs spread as we stood tightly embraced. The tight miniskirt she wore only aroused me more as I felt her long legs pressing against me. As my bone grew harder I pushed her back from me.

"Shit!" I cursed, "you talkin' 'bout not going shoppin'. If you kiss me like that again, we won't leave here for a couple of weeks."

Her beautiful eyes seemed to become smoky as she stared into mine. "That sounds fine to me, David, but those nosy bitches out at the pool were watching me so close when I came in that I would like to go back out as soon as possible so that their nasty little minds can't run amuck wondering what we are doing."

"Do you care?" I asked seriously.

"Not really," she replied quickly.

"Aw shit! Let's get that fuckin' shoppin' trip over with," I said quickly, now impatient to get her back and laid out on the water bed.

When we left my place, the women at the pool had been joined by two white dudes who stared at me angrily. I could see the anger in their eyes from where we walked, which was over fifty feet from the pool.

"I'm going to have to rent me a car so that I can get around," I told Janet as we reached the street.

"I see you're not planning on taking me up on my offer," she said, leading me over to the old 1961 Pontiac she drove. "Whenever you need transportation, it's here, though I realize it's not the latest model car on the road."

After she mentioned it, I remembered that she had offered to have a set of keys made for me last night. It had completely slipped my mind. "Naw, honey, it's nothing like that. Until I can find my way around, I might just take you up on the offer."

I found a pair of swimming trunks at the second store we entered, but by then I was caught up in the shopping spree. Two hours later we stopped at a restaurant and had a steak dinner with lobster. Now that's really a treat for a New Yorker. Imagine having lobster with steak for less than five dollars. Last, we both ordered Jello, which neither one of us had room for. But it was such a wonderful afternoon that neither one of us wanted to bring it to a close.

From what I'm writing here, you might get the impression that I was falling in love. Well, it wasn't no corny shit like that happening, it was just the newness of everything. Here I hadn't been in California three days, yet I had damn near copped me a white girl that looked like a movie star. Oh yeah, by the way, if I haven't mentioned it, I will now. Janet worked on a television show. Can you dig it? The bitch had got a job on TV.

We hadn't gotten around to rappin' on what kind of bread she made. She'd mentioned the fact to me that she worked on a program that came on once a week. I kind of faked her out when she mentioned it, you know. So what, big deal and all that shit, like it wasn't nothing, while all the time I was creamin' in my fuckin' pants. The bitch had to make fair paper no matter how small a part she had on the program.

Janet didn't drink, so I didn't really need any oil but I picked up a pint of gin anyway, just so that I would have it around the pad. Next, we went over to a friend of hers, and she ran in and bought, or they gave her, a bag of reefer.

"Oh shit!" she cried as we drove back to the motel. "I haven't got any papers, David." She took her eyes off her driving and glanced at me.

"Goddamn," I exploded as she nearly ran into an oncoming car, "don't get us killed over it. Just stop at the first drugstore you see, Janet, and I'll run in and pick up some."

I have to make a note of this since I'm from back east. They don't really have drugstores out here like we do back home. Mostly it's whiskey stores, unless you go to one of the large chainstore drugstores, yet it seems to work out okay.

We arrived at the motel and quickly got in the fuckin' bed. Ain't no sense me writing what all went down, 'cause then whoever ends up readin' this thing will think I was some kind of nut. What needs to be stated is the way she flipped over the heroin. Since it was China White, she couldn't tell the goddamn difference.

In a matter of minutes her head dropped down on her beautiful tits and she was in a dopefiend's nod. Then I watched her closely as she lifted her head and said, "Damn, Dave, this sure is some strong coke, honey. Maybe you should try cuttin' it more."

I had to fight back the laughter that came to my lips, it was going as sweet as I could possibly hope for it to go.

The dirty sonofabitch, Paul mumbled as he continued to read the diary. A loud disturbance in the hallway caused Paul to get up from his bed and open the door of his room. He watched the homosexual who stayed next door to him perform his weekly show. The sissy was completely naked except for a large butcher knife he held in his right hand. He was cursing at a tall dark-skinned man who Paul recognized as the homo's steady boyfriend. The tall dark young man was drunk, but not too drunk not to know the sissy had a knife.

As the homosexual's voice began to rise shrilly, Paul closed the door. He had seen this act too many times in the past. He knew that eventually the sissy would stop waving the knife or manage to run the tall man back into their small room and, after that, there would be the sounds of sex coming through the walls, with the sissy screaming out at the top of his voice in joy.

"What a fuckin' world," Paul whispered as he went back to the bed and picked up the diary again. For a minute he was tempted to put it down and go to sleep, but for some reason King David's poor attempt to really write a novel instead of a diary drew him to it. Somewhere in the back of his mind was the thought that it wouldn't take much to really put it in shape, not for him anyway.

If it remained interesting he just might make a complete book out of it. Of course, it would take some work, but a man didn't stumble over a good story every day, and from what he had read so far, it might just appeal to some sections of the public.

It's been over a week now since I've been giving Janet heroin for cocaine. She still doesn't know the difference. In fact, she has brought me another customer. A young white boy who is supposed to be some kind of director out at the studio where she works. At first, I was kind of leery of selling it to him, but it worked like a motherfuckin' charm. His name is Charles Bennett, a tall, long-haired bastard with a narrow face. He is as dumb as Janet is when it comes to dope. I've sold him heroin for coke, and all is well. So far, they haven't found out the difference, and by the time they do, I'll be out of the stuff.

Running out of dope. I'm shopping around trying to find a connection. Everybody out here says the Mexicans have the best dope, but since I don't speak Spanish, it's hard to make a connect. That's the only thing that's holding me back. If I can restock my supply of heroin, I might fuck around and get rich off these silly-ass peckerwoods.

Ran into a nigger up in Hollywood last night. I know he uses stuff, so I'm afraid to put my own money in his hand. He says he can cop me some raw stuff. That's what they call pure dope out here. It's supposed to be uncut. Uncut dope means you might be able to step on it two times if you are lucky.

But the way I see it, if I can find some good drugs and just step on it one time and it still be good, I'll clean up selling it to my white customers for coke. I'm going to meet the nigger at Club 21 this afternoon. Got to get dressed now so that I can take Janet to work. I'll need to use her raggedy-ass car the rest of the day.

Just the thought of Janet reminds me—the bitch is strung out just about as far as a bitch can get without really knowing it. I think she is beginning to realize it. She was sick yesterday morning, had to have some dope. Since she only snorts the stuff, it takes a hell of a lot of it to get her straightened out. Oh well, she has helped me out quite a bit, bringing me new customers and shit like that, so I don't mind giving the bitch credit whenever she asks for it. But my bag is gettin' damn near empty. If I should run out of stuff, the four honkies I got coppin' from me will realize that they are strung out, because every fuckin' one of them will end up sick as hell if I don't see to it that they get some drugs each and every day.

Well, that problem is over with now. I took the brother out to Watts. Goddamn, but it's a fuckin' ghetto out there. It looks like something out of Mississippi. All they got is small-ass houses, with niggers hangin' out on every corner. Yet I felt at home while out there. I guess it just shows that you can take a nigger out of the country but you can't get the country out of a nigger.

I wouldn't let the brother out of my sight with the money, so he had to take me in and introduce me to his goddamn connect. He told the man we were brothers, real ones at that. The nigger went along with it anyway and sold me some drugs. I let my junkie test the dope for me after I just put one on it.

Even after the nigger swore I could put two on it, I still just cut it one time. It's good dope with one cut of mix on it. I'm going to have to use a lot of milk sugar to get it as white as I want it to be so that it can pass for cocaine. I spent one hundred and fifty dollars for a quarter piece of raw dope. Didn't cut but one fifty-dollar raw balloon, savin' the rest until I got back to my place so that I could put the milk sugar on it, plus the rest of the white dope I got. Had I been thinkin' before, I would have copped sooner. That way, I could have used my China White dope to cut the dark brown shit they sell out here for heroin.

Had a hard time gettin' rid of the nigger who took me out to Watts. He wanted to follow me home, like I was fool enough to let a nigger like that know where I stay. I had to threaten to put my foot in his ass if he didn't get out of the car when I got back to Hollywood. Promised him that, whenever I get ready to cop, I'll call him up so he can go along and test my dope for me.

So it ain't just a lie I told him; I might just really need him. Took his phone number just in case. Somebody has to test this shit, 'cause I sure in the hell ain't about to. I got to respect King Heroin. Seen it knock too many boss players on their ass for me to ever make the mistake and put the needle in my arm even one more time. As the dope-fiends say, once is too many, a thousand times is not enough. I believe them; they should know. Heroin is to be sold, not used.

Well, happy days are here. Just gave Janet a free sample of my new batch. The ignorant bitch loved it. Just goes to show you, people love that which they can't control. Anyway, I fixed up eight twenty-five-dollar balloons for Janet to take along with her to work. She sold at least two hundred dollars worth of dope a day at the studio for me. It was one hell of a set-up I had going. String out half the honkies that work on a daily television show.

Sometimes I watch the show and try to figure out which of the white actors are junkies. I know at least four of them are. The sight of them tickles the shit out of me, because I know I can bring their little play-house crumbling down around their fuckin' heads whenever I feel like pulling the string.

Paul closed the diary slowly, shaking his head. What kind of a sonofabitch was King David, he wondered, as he stretched out on the bed and tried to find some sleep. But sleep didn't come quickly. The words in the diary kept coming back to him, and he realized he wanted to know why King David was killed.

8

MOON DIDN'T HAVE long to wait after the men left before he had more company. Alvin came through the door, followed by Rockie. Rockie's dark face lit up with a smile as he pulled out the envelope and held it out to Moon. "Them niggers ran into more trouble than they were lookin' for," he said as Moon took the money from him.

Moon glared at his lieutenant. "Them niggers don't know what the meaning of trouble is yet!"

Rockie glanced over at Alvin. They had discussed it in the car. Alvin had stated that Moon would end up knockin' all three of them off, but Rockie hadn't believed it.

After counting the money quickly, Moon managed to get his temper under control. "It's a goddamn shame Mike couldn't forget the old problems—or better yet, handled the fuckin' hit cleanly. Then it wouldn't be all this shit. Now us three have got to get the hell out of here. I want some kind of alibi in case something should happen this evening and people get to wonderin' where the fuck was old Moon. So I reckon you boys had better have a good alibi, too."

Moon glanced at his two men, then put the clincher on it. "I don't really need one, but you boys might just need one, so I'm going to take you out on the town." He laughed loudly. "I don't reckon we'll need any hardware on us. Just in case some of them fuckin' detectives try playing at being police officers tonight, we won't give them the chance to make no cases on us." Moon laughed again loudly, then reached out and patted Rockie on the back.

Both men walked over to the bar, taking the pistols with them. Alvin went behind the bar and opened the panel. He shoved both guns in, then came back around the bar.

Moon grinned at him like a happy father. "Good, now let's ride over to Sonny Wilson's joint. There should be some fine brown-skinned broads layin' around doing nothin' who would just love our company." Moon led the way toward the door.

Before Moon could reach the door, Alvin ran around him to open it. Alvin held the door open until Rockie and Moon had gone through. They took the elevator downstairs. Once outside, Alvin again held the door open, this time it was the door of Moon's private limousine. The large luxury automobile was designed in such a way that only a chauffeur looked right driving it.

As Moon settled himself comfortably in the backseat, Alvin got in the front on the passenger side, and Rockie took over as chauffeur. The big motor started up quickly, purring the way only an expensive car motor can. As Rockie pulled away from the curb, Moon reached over and opened up the small refrigerator bar in the back of his car. He quickly mixed himself a shot of scotch on the rocks. He tossed it off and fixed another one. This one he took his time with, settling back against the leather and enjoying the ride. As they went down the darkened ghetto streets, people out walking glanced curiously at the expensive car that passed them by.

Their destination was down in Harlem. Rockie drove through the light traffic expertly, weaving the long automobile in and out of the traffic. In a few minutes he pulled up in front of a nightclub that had seen better days.

Alvin got out of the car first. He didn't like the idea of being weaponless, but Moon was the boss. He glanced up and down the street closely before stepping to the back door and opening it for Moon.

The few idle strollers walking past didn't slow down to look. One glance at the passengers in the car was enough for them. In Harlem you didn't see expensive cars like the long black one at the curb unless it was loaded with gangsters.

Rich white people didn't dare venture into that

part of the black ghetto at night, so the only other persons able to afford such autos were the crooks and the politicians, who were just as crooked as the gangsters.

As Alvin held the rear door open, Moon climbed out of the backseat. He moved the way most fat men moved—slowly and ponderously. His heavy belly shook as he straightened up and glanced around.

Five young teenagers stopped and watched the big dope man as he made his way across the sidewalk and into the nightclub. It would be something for them to talk about the next day. It wasn't every day that they got a chance to see the biggest dealer in the district. They watched the way Moon's two lieutenants handled themselves, opening the doors in front of him and searching the surroundings for danger. There was no pretense. The two gunmen were extra serious because they didn't have any guns on them. The thought of danger leaping out at them was always present. It would be a good time for a rival dealer to get Moon out of the way.

The inside of the club was dark. A light-complexioned woman hurried over and met them at the door. She smiled brightly, revealing marvelous teeth. "Why, Mister Moon, what a wonderful surprise. Why didn't you call? We could have saved your favorite table for you."

Moon grinned at her. "Thanks, Brenda, but it's not necessary. We didn't even know we were going to drop by tonight. We were on this side of town, so I decided to stop by and hear your latest singer. I've heard she was real good." Moon peered down at the low-cut gown she wore. Her lush breasts seemed about to pop out of the tight-fitting dress.

Brenda knew that Moon liked her. Every time the gangster visited, he gave her a good tip. As she led them to the best table she could find she noticed that he was already digging around in his pocket for her tip. When she reached the closest table she could find near the stage, she stopped and smiled.

"I'm sorry, sir, but if I'd only known, I would have kept you a better one open all night." She made the statement only to insure a larger tip.

Moon smiled at her. He liked the attention he got when they walked into the club. He knew everybody in the place was watching them. "If Mister Wilson isn't too busy," he said loudly, "tell him I'm here and, if he has the time, to come on over and have a drink with me."

Brenda continued to hold her bright smile, even as she wished he would lower his voice. She knew better than to insult someone like Moon. That could become very bad business. In fact, it could even cost Brenda her job. Moon carried quite a bit of weight and it wasn't just his body.

"He's back in his office going over some books, but I will make sure he gets your message, dear," Brenda said lightly. She took the twenty-dollar bill out of his hand as he held it out to her.

Moon settled down in his chair with his broad back against the nearby wall. All three of the men kept their eyes on Brenda's large ass as she made her way through the tables. She was an eyeful, and just about every man inside the club watched her as she walked.

Her body swayed as though she was keeping up with some music that no one heard but her. It was graceful, not faked. Her hips moved, but it seemed more a part of her than something she had practiced for hours until she had perfected it. Only Brenda knew how many painful hours she had spent walking up and down a stairway with some books on her head, while she kept her back perfectly straight. It was part of her makeup. She wanted to be a lady, and everybody who met her came away with just that opinion. She was one hell of a lady.

The waitress rushed up to Moon's table. "Bring us a bottle of Sonny's best champagne, honey," Moon ordered quickly. The men watched her ass as she walked away. The tight shorts she wore covered little, exposing a good portion of her ass.

Rockie broke out into a grin. "Now I'd like to ride that for a few hours."

"Your ass," Alvin said. "The only thing you'd like to do would be to lay your fuckin' head up between them hips, boy, and cool it off."

"I been hearing you're one hell of a cocksucker, Rockie, my boy. Now I know you ain't no bushwhacker, is you?" Moon was joking, and Alvin broke out into loud laughter.

Rockie grinned sheepishly. "Ain't no walls talked yet, Moon." The three men laughed good-naturedly, then turned toward an attractive woman who had just walked onto the stage.

The woman made a few good jokes about the crowd, then started to sing in a deep, sexy voice. She sang some blues, then quickly moved into a beautiful rendition of "Over the Rainbow." The crowd fell silent as she sang. When she finished, they broke into loud clapping and stomping, yelling for more. She finally agreed to sing one more number.

"Goddamn, that gal can sing!" Moon said as the singer finished and left the stage. He waved toward a waitress, beckoning for the woman to hurry over. "Honey," he said as she came up to the table, "you go back to the office and tell Mister Wilson that Mister Moon would like to see him as soon as possible, you understand?"

"I'm sorry," the young waitress said quickly, "but I'm not allowed to go back to the office."

"Hey, hey, honey. Do you know who that is you're talkin' to?" Alvin asked sharply.

"No," the girl answered honestly, "but it doesn't make any difference. I'm still not allowed to go back to Mister Wilson's office unless he asks for me."

Moon rubbed his chin thoughtfully. "Okay, gal, I'll tell you what, you go find Brenda. You go find her and tell her to get over here real quick. Now, do you think you're allowed to do something like that?"

The young waitress shifted around nervously. "Yes, I can do that," she said finally. Then before either of the men could say anything else, she hurried off. When she saw Brenda near the cloak room she almost broke into a run.

"Brenda," she yelled as she came near, "you better go over to that table where the fat man is at. He's demanding that someone go back and get Mister Wilson for him."

"That's okay, Jean," Brenda answered quickly, "I told Moon when I took him to his seat that I would inform Mister Wilson that he was here."

"Well, he just asked me to ask you to come back over to his table. He wants to see you right now. Though I don't know who in the hell he thinks he is, giving people orders like he owns the place." The waitress was belligerent, unaware of either Moon's importance or his bankroll.

"Well, don't worry about him," Brenda said quietly, "though he could cause you more trouble than you want. Just leave him to me. You have to handle Mister Moon with kid gloves, Jean."

"Well, I'm glad you're handling him instead of me," Jean said. "Something about him gives me the creeps."

Brenda laughed as she walked away. When she noticed all of the men at Moon's table watching her, she hurried toward them. "Yes sir, can I be of any help?" she asked brightly.

"Yeah," Moon said, "I wanted to talk to Wilson. But now I've had a better idea. I want to have a few words with that singer. Do you think you could get her to come over to the table and have a drink with us?"

She bent down before answering. This was going to be a problem, she reflected coldly as she made sure Moon had a good look at her semi-exposed tits. "Moon, honey," she began, "that's a problem there." She held up her hand before Moon could say anything. "Nancy, our singer, is married to a very jealous man. She never joins anybody at their table. Keeps the confusion down at home." Brenda laughed to take the sting out of her words. "I don't know why the dude is so jealous, though; she's got four kids and don't no man want no woman with four kids by somebody else. You know what I mean?"

With the utmost patience, Moon waited until she had finished her little speech. "You don't seem to understand, Brenda. I'm not out shopping around for some stray cunt. In fact, if that was what I wanted, I wouldn't even have to leave my penthouse; it would be delivered. And it would be the best on the market. No, that's not it. I want to talk to the little singer about a business propo-sition."

"Oh!" Brenda managed to say before she was cut off.

"Don't worry about it," Moon said generously. "We all have the propensity to go off half-cocked at times. Now would you be so kind, Brenda, as to ask the young lady over so that I can inquire about the chance of both of us making some green stuff?"

Damn! Brenda cursed under her breath. There was no way she could get out of approaching Nancy, even though she had a good idea what Nancy would say. Nancy didn't want anything to do with some neighborhood gangster, no matter how much pull he might have in this small world.

But she knew it wasn't her place to tell him that. Mister Wilson could easily replace her, yet he'd think twice before attempting to replace Nancy. She was more than just good, she was exceptional.

"Well, Moon, since you put it that way, I'll relay your wishes to Nancy. But I still can't promise anything. If I can't get her to come, I'll relay your message to Mister Wilson and see if he can do it." Brenda turned away from the table and hurried backstage.

As she made her way through the tables, Brenda decided that, whatever happened, she would make sure she came out of it smelling like a rose. Nancy was a hard rock to crack, and she didn't have any idea about how the singer might react. She walked past the stage and entered the narrow hallway that led back to the dressing rooms and the boss' office. There was a faded gold star painted on the door that led into the singer's dressing room. Brenda knocked loudly, then when she heard Nancy asking who it was, she entered.

"Hi, Nancy," Brenda said as she closed the dressing room door behind her. She glanced around the room. Gowns were everywhere—on the chair, on the large suitcase sitting against the brightly painted yellow wall. Brenda was a constant visitor backstage, so Nancy just smiled when she saw who it was. The two women sometimes rode home together because Nancy didn't have a car.

"Hi, Brenda, what brings you back this way? Searching for a good drink?" Nancy pointed to a pint of whiskey sitting on the dresser. "Help yourself, ain't no fuckin' ice, though. I can't get one of those lazy-ass bitches to bring me none back here."

"Naw, sugar," Brenda said quickly. "I got a problem, honey."

"What's that?" Nancy inquired good-naturedly.

"Shit!" Brenda said, pushing some clothes off a chair onto the floor and flopping down into the chair.

"Have a seat," Nancy said sarcastically as she saw her dresses shoved so coldly onto the floor. If Brenda hadn't pushed them onto the floor, Nancy would have done the same thing. To see someone else push her dresses on the floor kind of rubbed her the wrong way.

"My, my, aren't we in a good temper tonight," Brenda said as she crossed her legs and lit a cigarette.

For a moment the two women stared at each other, then Nancy reached over and poured herself a drink. Brenda watched as the brown-skinned singer drained the whiskey straight, then poured another. Without all the makeup, Brenda could see the lines in Nancy's face. She knew that she was not a young woman any longer. Nancy was in her late thirties and the heavy drinking showed. There were bags under her eyes from too many late hours and too much whiskey.

"What's worrying you, Brenda?" Nancy asked in a mellow voice.

Brenda let out a sigh. The best way to get to the solution of her problem would be with the truth. Any other way would be a waste of time. "Nancy, I got a fuckin' problem, and it concerns you," Brenda said, glancing around for somewhere to knock her ashes and finding a crowded ashtray on the edge of the trunk.

The two women became silent while they eyed each other. "Well," Nancy said, "you're going to have to explain that a littl' more clearly, Brenda, 'cause I sure as hell don't know where you're comin' from."

Clenching her jaw, Brenda blurted out the truth. "Nancy, I got a petty gangster outside sittin' at ringside. I guess you know him. Moon, the big dope man from uptown?" Brenda spread out her hands, then cut Nancy off with a wave and continued. "He heard you sing and now he wants me to get you to join him at his table."

"The hell he do!" Nancy yelled. "You know I don't sit at no bastard's table, Brenda!"

"I know, I know," Brenda answered quickly. "I told the motherfucker just that, Nancy, but you know how these neighborhood gangsters are. They got so much pride and think everybody should jump when they speak 'cause they have a pocketful of money. He don't want to talk bullshit with you. He says to tell you he can help you cut a record."

"Yeah, I just bet he can," Nancy said quickly.

"Naw, honey, it ain't no bullshit!" Brenda said. "If Moon says he can do it, he can. He's not trying to hit on you either, I give you my word on that. He says to let you know that it's strictly money he's interested in. Nothing else."

"You believe this creep?" Nancy asked, her curiosity rising.

"Oh yeah. It's no doubt about that part of it. I just figured you might not want to be involved with no fuckin' gangster. Moon's big, I mean real big, Nancy. Cuttin' a record wouldn't be no problem."

Nancy stood up and tossed the whiskey off. "Shit! I don't give a damn if it's the devil, if he can help me get a few motherfuckin' numbers out, sure I'll talk to him. Hell, he can't be worse than them fuckin' honkies uptown who want to take all the money. Sure, kid, don't worry about it; let's go out and see what this big daddy really has to say."

Brenda was surprised but she wouldn't show it. She stood up quickly and led the way out, wondering how easy it was to go through life thinking you knew somebody, then find out you didn't really know a goddamn thing about them. She would have bet money that Nancy wouldn't want anything to do with a hoodlum, yet here she was, actually in a hurry to get out and meet a gangster who might be able to help her.

9

———

A S THE TRIO SAT in the garage waiting for Moon's men to show up and take Blue to the doctor, Blue began to moan loudly.

"Maybe it would be better if you got some cold water and washed his face," Edna said worriedly, staring at the hurt man. "Damn, Mike, it don't look like he's goin' live, if you ask me."

"I ain't heard nobody ask you," Mike stated coldly. But even as he said the words, he opened the car door and got out. He searched around the rear of the garage looking for somewhere to get some water. Just when he was about to give up the search and go up and inquire as to the whereabouts of the toilet, he saw a door with a faded sign over it. He pushed it open, noticing that the men inside the office were involved in something. Both of their heads were down.

The inside of the tiny bathroom was filthy. Mike ignored the dirty tissue on the floor and the pool of stinking piss where someone had completely disregarded the upright basin. He searched diligently but still couldn't find anything to put water in.

The hell with it, he told himself, growing tired of the fruitless search. He attempted to cup his hands and carry some water that way, but when he got to the door, he couldn't get it open without using one of his hands. The water ran down through his open fingers, causing him to curse loudly. Opening the door, he let it slam loudly, then began to make his way back toward the parked car.

As he came between two cars he saw the back door open and three men come through. He instantly recognized the men. The quiet way they moved toward the car put him on his guard.

Mike couldn't reason it out, but the men seemed too sneaky. He moved slowly and unseen toward the car. As he drew closer, he noticed that one of the gunmen had a shotgun clutched tightly in his hand. If Mike had been inside the car he never would have noticed it, but from where he crouched, he could see everything about the men. The man with the sawed-off shotgun held it down against his leg.

The three gunmen quickly surrounded the car. Edna glanced up as the men peeped in through the window. The friendly greeting died in her throat. There was something about the men that fright-

ened her, even though none of them had made a
menacing motion toward her.

One of the men glanced in the window at Blue.
Then he opened the car door on the passenger
side. "Shit!" he exclaimed. "Blue don't need nothing but some buryin'!" He then raised his gun and
pulled the trigger. The sound of the gun going off
inside the building rang out loudly.

"You stupid sonofabitch," the other gunman
yelled out, snatching open the door on Edna's side.

"What's going on?" Edna screamed. But she
was cut off when the man raised a small handgun
and fired twice. The heavy slugs plowed into the
young girl's face, spattering blood all over the car
seat. The force of the bullets knocked her completely over. She slid down the car seat and out
the open passenger door. Her body fell on top of
Blue's blood-soaked body.

A scream of angry rage and pain filled the
building. Mike came roaring around the parked
car with a .38 spitting fire. His first bullet took
Duke in the face. The man fell back without making a sound. Mike screamed out at the top of his
voice. "Edna! Edna! You dirty motherfuckers!"

At first Earl and Red had been taken by surprise, but both men were experts. They quickly
got themselves together.

Earl had been searching for Mike. The young
man was his personal target. He raised the shotgun quickly and pulled the trigger on one barrel.
The blast from the gun was loud but not deadly.

Mike had just seen his sister's body and, at the time Earl pressed down on the trigger, he leaped forward to see if she was still alive. Part of the shotgun blast took him in the side.

As Mike was about to reach down and snatch his sister's body up, the blow hit him. The force of the shotgun blast slammed him into the parked car next to his. He bounced off the car and quickly raised the pistol in his hand.

Earl ran around the car with the sawed-off shotgun leveled out straight. He wanted a better shot this time. As soon as he came around the fender of the car, Mike pulled the trigger. Two slugs from the .38 automatic slammed into Earl's chest. He was stopped in his tracks as if he had run straight into a brick wall.

Mike's thin lips were formed in a grimace of pain, but he kept his feet under him. Rage filled him with a fighting spirit that he ordinarily would not have had. Out of the corner of his eye, he saw Red aiming the sawed-off shotgun at him over the front of the car's hood. Mike dove wildly for the pavement as the shotgun blast went off. The pellets from the cartridge tore into the parked car behind him but missed his moving body.

Suddenly it dawned on Red that he had used up both shotgun shells. He tossed the useless weapon aside and broke for the back door.

Mike, lying on the pavement, saw the shotgun hit the concrete. The next thing he noticed was

Red's flashing feet as the man dashed for the back door.

Fighting back a sob as he stood up, Mike braced his elbows on the top of the car hood and took careful aim. He steadied the pistol in both hands, then squeezed off a shot. The first bullet took Red high in the back but didn't stop him. He stumbled once, then continued to run. Mike again took deadly aim and slowly pulled the trigger. This time there was an empty click as the gun came around on an empty chamber.

For a second Mike stared around wildly, then he saw Blue at his feet. He reached down and shoved his sister's body off the dead man and searched frantically for the man's weapon. He re-membered suddenly that Blue wore a small belt holster. He opened the dead man's coat and snatched out the deadly .38.

Red didn't know how he made it. All the time he was spending trying to get the door open, he expected to feel the shock of another bullet in his back, but it didn't come. He managed to snatch the rear door open and fall through. The small paved steps that he had come up so easily now tripped him up. He grabbed the arm rail and strug-gled down the stairs. When he reached the bot-tom he raised his hand and waved for Charlie in the car. He knew he was hit and hit bad. He couldn't control his feet. His mind was still functioning and he knew if he could only make the car every-thing would be all right.

Mike ran for the rear door. He glanced over his shoulder once and thought he saw people at the front of the garage staring back at him, but he couldn't be sure. The pain in his shoulder didn't bother him too much. When he thought of his sister lying there with blood all over her the pain disappeared altogether. He had trouble getting the back door open, but he managed to finally wrench it.

The pain from his wound made him hesitate before he staggered to the steps to look for his wounded prey. Red had managed to get away from the rear of the building, yet he still hadn't been able to get the driver of the car to see him. It was too dark in the alley for a person to see more than a few feet in front of him. For the moment that helped save Red's life, because Mike couldn't see him in the darkness.

As Red stumbled along, he fell into the nearby wall of another building. As he bounced back, he knocked over two garbage cans. The sounds of the cans falling over did more for Mike than anything else. He couldn't quite make out Red in the darkness, but he had an idea of where the man was. The sound of Red's breathing came to him suddenly, and he knew the man couldn't be too far ahead of him.

Mike forced himself down the short steps and ran in the direction of the noise. As he stumbled along trying to run, the sound of his feet put fear in Red's heart. Now that Red could hear Mike behind him, he tossed all caution to the wind.

"Charlie, Charlie," he screamed in a shrill voice, trying to run. "Goddamn it, Charlie, help me!" The sound of the terrified man helped Mike out. He knew now that the one he sought couldn't be far ahead. Also, he became aware of the fact that there was another man. Mike shifted the .38 in his hand and continued on, staring intently into the darkness ahead of him.

Suddenly he saw something. He raised the gun and fired. "Oh my God!" Red screamed. The bullets buzzed past his frightened head.

The sound of the gunshots caused Charles to snap to attention. He cut on the headlights of the car and instantly illuminated Red stumbling through the darkness. "Goddamn," Charles cursed under his breath, "I thought this was supposed to be a cakewalk." He started the car up quickly, to go after Red.

Charles shifted the car into gear and drove toward the running figure. In his fear, Red didn't know which side of the car to run to. He staggered up to the driver's side.

Charles cursed. "Goddamn it, Red, how the fuck are you supposed to get in?" He jumped from behind the steering wheel so that Red could get into the car. But Red never made it. From out of the darkness another figure appeared.

I can't let the bastards get away, Mike told himself as he stared through the blackness and finally saw the parked car. He pulled himself up from the stumbling run he had been in. As the driver jumped out of the car to let Red in, Mike took careful aim.

His first shot struck Charles in the shoulder, spinning the man around.

Charles cursed loudly. "I'm hit, Red," he yelled as he fumbled for his gun. Red let out a scream of pure panic and started to run past the car. "Why, you dirty sonofabitch," Charles yelled after the fleeing figure, then raised his pistol and shot Red in the back.

This time the blow struck Red between the shoulderblades and knocked him completely off his feet. As he fell onto his face in the alley, the gun battle continued.

Mike, seeing the flash of the gun, raised his pistol and again took careful aim. This time the bullet struck Charles in the left arm, again spinning him around. Charles cursed but managed to stay on his feet. He ripped off two quick shots into the darkness, not sure of where his enemy was.

Again the gun flashes revealed Charles' whereabouts to the hunter. Mike fired twice more as he advanced on the wounded man. He heard the man grunt, then the sound of a body hitting the ground. He stalked slowly toward the car. He came around the front of it and made his way to the rear, where he found Charles' body. The man was stretched out on his back, with his pistol still in his hand.

Mike bent down and removed the gun from Charles' hand. His own pain was so sharp that he had trouble straightening up. He leaned against the car until he got control of himself, then staggered to the open door of the car.

Red could feel the life draining out of his body as he started to crawl. He needed a doctor badly, if he was to retain any hope of making it. The pain in his back was so bad that he didn't think he would be able to make it, but he had to try. The smell of the garbage came to him, and he closed his eyes and prayed for the strength to make it. Somebody had to have heard the sounds of the shoot-out, so help would be coming. All he had to do was hold on until that help came. God, he prayed, he didn't want to die alone in the alley. Don't let me go like this, Lord, please. The sound of the racing car engine came to him, and for a moment he thought that Charles was coming to get him.

Red tried to call out to Charles as the car backed toward him. "Here, Charlie," he yelled, but his voice was barely a whisper. He twisted his neck around and tried to see. The last thing he saw was the rear end of the automobile bearing down on him. His scream wasn't even heard by the man driving the car.

Mike felt the bump as he backed over Red but couldn't figure out what he had hit until his lights picked up the dead man. When he saw the body, Mike shifted the car gears and drove straight back over the body, then backed up once more.

People standing at the mouth of the alley saw everything that happened from the weak street-lamp that stood a few feet away. As the car came backing out of the alley, they scattered like birds in a field at the approach of a hunter.

Hunched over the steering wheel, Mike fought off the pain. He merely wanted to exist now for vengeance. Pain meant nothing, he told himself over and over again. Whenever he began to feel weak, he saw the image of Edna, lying bloody on the garage floor. It was more than enough to chase the pain away. The thought of the man who had sent the killers became a malignant growth inside of him. There had been no reason for it, he told himself. Then Mike started to remember their conversation, and he realized that Moon had been planning on killing them all the time he talked on the phone. That was the reason he had asked Mike to make sure Edna stayed there until they arrived. Even then he had been planning the death of his kid sister.

When the thought flashed through Mike's mind, he had to fight off the enveloping reddish haze of madness. He struggled to control himself so that he could drive the car. Mike realized suddenly that he had just run a red light. That wouldn't do, he warned himself. He couldn't stand to be stopped before he finished this night's work. No matter what happened, he'd have to reach Moon's place.

Somehow he managed to reach his destination without being stopped. He parked the car down the street, away from the streetlight. The neighborhood he was now in was above average. He was on Park Avenue, and most of the apartment buildings had well-lighted entrances.

No matter how much it took, Mike told himself, he would be able to do it. He carefully checked the loads in both weapons. He only had two bullets in one gun and three in the other one. Both pistols were .38s. He took the bullets out of one and reloaded the other pistol. Now that he had five bullets, he believed it would be more than enough to take care of what he had to do.

10

IT WAS NO USE, Paul finally decided. He switched on the lamp beside the bed, glancing at the small clock on the dresser. It was just three o'clock in the morning, yet he couldn't sleep. All night long he hadn't been able to think about anything but what was in the diary. Well, he decided as he kicked the sheets off his body and sat up, if he couldn't sleep because of the diary, he might as well spend the rest of the night reading it so that he wouldn't have the same problem tomorrow night.

The first thing he did after getting up was recheck his coffee pot. He hadn't drunk all of the coffee, so he quickly lit the burners under it and reheated what he had left in the pot. Paul's mind was in an uproar. This was the first time anything had ever affected him in such a manner. Not sleeping was one problem he rarely had.

As he poured his cupful of steaming coffee, he

stopped for a second and listened closely to the loud noise coming from downstairs. Now that is really rude, he told himself. Anybody stupid enough to play their radio that loud at this time of night, either is the most stupid person or one of the most rude you would ever meet. In this case, he reasoned, the foolish woman under him was mixed with both stupidity and rudeness.

Angered by the woman's unreasonableness, Paul raised his foot and stomped loudly on the floor. As pain shot up through his foot, he realized that he hadn't put his shoes on. He reached under the bed and slipped them on, then he stomped around for a few minutes as loudly as he could. If she was asleep, she would wake up. For his behavior, the woman turned the radio up even louder.

"You win, stupid bitch," Paul groaned as he fixed his coffee. After getting his cup he carried it back over to the bed. He had to grin slyly as he thought about it. She had turned her radio up so loud now that he was sure he wasn't the only person she was disturbing. Actually, she wasn't bothering him, because in a few seconds he'd be so involved with the diary it wouldn't be heard by him. The sound of someone else knocking loudly on the wall trying to make her turn it down caused Paul to smile. In another second, he was so absorbed in the diary that the radio and coffee were both forgotten.

I have bought me an old 1964 Cadillac, and moved into an apartment. I had to cut down on the rent some kind of way. Even though it didn't bother me because I'm making money hand over fist. But I wanted to be away from Janet's friends and customers; since all of them had known I stayed at the motel, it was time to leave. The apartment building I stay in has a pool too, so I won't miss the swimming. It's one of the few things I really have to do. Must find something else to do to help kill the time. The dope is selling like hotcakes like always. By now, all of the white kids have got habits, but that is their problem, not mine. I've made over five thousand dollars so far, so things are beginning to look up.

King David's next entry carried a date.

Now that I've been on the West Coast for a year I feel like I was born out here. I've still got Janet even though she has lost her job. Some kind of way they found out she was a junkie and discharged her, but that was all right with me. Now I use her to sell dope for me on a full-time basis. She is one hell of a good dope dealer. She has finally found out that it ain't coke that she has been using. She called me a black motherfucker, so I had to kick her white ass for her, but everything is all right now. I won't let the bitch live with me though. In fact, I don't even enjoy taking the junkie-ass bitch to bed no more. But I keep my feelings hid, I still need her white ass, so I'm not about to get rid of something as good as she is.

Goddamn! Today I ran into the finest black chick I've ever met. The bitch was tall, with a complexion like coffee with plenty of cream in it. Her skin is so smooth that I couldn't hardly keep my hands off her. I ran into her at a party up in Hollywood. She had come along with some stiff-ass nigger, so I couldn't pull the bitch when I left. But I did manage to cop on her that, if she liked to get froze, to get in touch. I left her with my phone number, and knowing bitches, they all like a little coke now and then. It makes them freakish, so they say, but if the truth was known, they were freakish before they ever snorted cocaine.

My phone just rang and, just like I thought, it was this tall bundle of joy. Just over twenty years old, a little taller than five foot six, under a hundred and twenty-five pounds, with a body that God had built for only one purpose, which I'm going to check out real damn soon.

My dream girl showed up just like she promised, wearing a form-fitting knitted dress that showed them big buns that I got into a little later on. But I still can't get over that heart-shaped face with the carmine mouth and huge black eyes that can be only called bedroom eyes. She had that pile of black hair that at first I thought was a wig, but after we got in the sack I found out that it was her real hair.

My God but making love to her was a joy. And I really gave her some real old-fashioned dickin'. At one time I was tempted to suck that old tight pussy 'cause it was the best ass I've ever had. Now when I look back at what I've wrote, I'm not ashamed. At the present time I don't know where our relationship is going, but this is the first woman I've ever met that I didn't want to play on. If things keep on going along like they are, I think I'm going to let Juanita move in with me.

The next entry in the diary was a week later. This was the first time King David had ever used red ink.

Today I offered Juanita the opportunity to move in with me. This would be a chance for her to better her condition and really get on her feet, because I'm making money so fast that at times I'm scared. I hate to keep large sums of money around, though few people know where I live.

It's still hard for me to believe but the silly-ass bitch turned me down. She really turned me down. When I asked why, she said she didn't like the way I earned my living. Can you dig that? Here's a silly bitch who snorts up every drop of coke I put in front of her, yet she doesn't like the way I earn my living. How the hell she thinks I can afford the cocaine I give her every day is beyond me.

I guess she takes it for damn granted. Now I am sure women don't think, I mean they don't use their brains like a man. They think with their pussy. That's where their brain is located at. It couldn't be anywhere else. Between their legs, nowhere else. Again I offered her the chance to move in with me. Again she turned me down, yet she still gives me all the pussy I can handle.

King David's next entry revealed his anger.

I'm sick and tired now of playing with Juanita. The silly bitch has got my nose open. I hope to be able to shake this feeling; I've never experienced it before. I've heard niggers talk about being in love, even writing the word makes me feel simple, but it's true. I have never felt this way about another person other than my mother in my life. And I don't like it. I mean it from the bottom of my heart; I detest this feeling of concern I have for Juanita. It makes me feel like I'm weak.

After reading this page of the diary, Paul reached for his coffee and drained the cup of cold liquid before turning to it again. He couldn't believe what he was reading. Could a man really feel this way, he wondered. Could another human being really hate the human race enough not to want to accept love when it came to him? A man who was lucky enough to meet a woman that he really cared for and then purposely go out of his way and fight against human nature. Paul shook his head. It was unbelievable.

King David was leaving the realm of reality as far as Paul was concerned. Now he had to wonder if what he read in the diary was true or not. Yes, he reflected as he thought about the matter, it was true. That was one of the reasons King David had written the diary, Paul believed. The man was trying to face himself, trying to justify a reason for his being alive.

Before he could read any further, he was distracted by angry voices out in the hallway. He didn't have to open his door to hear them, but he did anyway. That way the words were clearer. Paul leaned in his doorway, listening; the argument was coming from downstairs.

"Goddamn you!" It was a man's angry voice. "I asked you like a gentleman to turn that fuckin' radio down," the man yelled, "but no, a person can't treat you like a lady and give you a little respect. Hell no, if they do that, your dumb ass will take kindness for weakness. Now I asked you nicely, black-ass bitch, to turn that muthabuggerin' cocksuckin' radio down, yet you wouldn't pay no attention to me. Now you ignorant, black bitch, I ain't askin', you dig? I'm tellin' you, whore,

if you don't do somethin' 'bout that muthafucker,
I'm personally goin' kick your thin-ass door down
and come in. Now, bitch, if I have to go to that
much trouble, I'm sho' 'nuff goin' step off in your
ass. So please take a warnin', crazy-ass bitch, 'cause
I ain't goin' warn you again!"

Paul glanced at his wristwatch. It was ten minutes to four. The angry man must have listened to
it for a long time before deciding to go downstairs
to her door. Without seeing who the foul-mouthed
man was, Paul knew him. It was the new tenant
who stayed across the hall from Paul. Even as he
thought about who it was, he glanced over in time
to see the man's wife come out of their room carrying the young baby. Her face was twisted up in a
frown. Paul instantly realized what must have happened. The loud music probably woke the child
up. The sound of the baby crying had then awakened the parents.

The thin, dark-skinned woman usually spoke
whenever she saw Paul, but this time she stalked
to the head of the stairway without so much as
nodding in his direction.

"Jimmy, Jimmy," she called out in a pleading
voice, "don't get into no trouble because of that
silly-ass bitch."

As far as Paul was concerned, the couple seemed
to be nice people. They rarely made noise in their
apartment and seemed generally friendly. This was
the first time Paul had ever heard the man raise
his voice. Most of the time he was a soft-spoken

man, even though he did look quite fierce with his heavy black mustache and thick beard.

From the tone of the man's voice, there was no doubt in Paul's mind that the man was serious. He didn't seem like the kind of person who would make idle threats. As Paul listened, the radio went down in volume, showing that he wasn't the only one who took the man at his word. Paul didn't know how long it would last, but he was thankful for the temporary relief they would get from the woman. For the moment she was scared, and Paul could only hope it would last until he was lucky enough to find himself another apartment. Since receiving the money, he had dwelled on the idea of finding another place. Once he finished paying out the money for the burial, he would be sure to have enough left over to finance the expenses of moving. It would be completely out of this district, he reflected. He owed himself that much. Maybe with a change of neighborhoods his luck might change and a publisher would buy another one of his novels.

The heavyset dark-skinned man came up the steps. He stopped when he saw his wife standing at the head of the stairway. "The baby ain't gone back to sleep yet, huh?" he inquired in a deep voice.

The woman shook her head. "Jimmy, I don't want you gettin' in no trouble over that woman here. No tellin' how your parole officer might take a disturbance like this. Shit, Jimmy, you know they don't need much of an excuse to send you back. . . ."

Before she could finish, the man cut her off. "Why don't you watch what you're saying, woman? Everybody's business ain't nobody's business," he stated as he clutched her arm tightly and damn near pointed at Paul standing in the doorway.

The woman quickly got the message. She shut her mouth so hard that Paul believed he could hear her teeth click. He felt foolish now, knowing that the man hadn't wanted him to know about the parole, even though he didn't give a shit about it one way or the other. But since he was white, the only white person besides the faggot in the whole apartment building, he was under suspicion. Half of the people believed he was a police officer, while the other half thought he was a junkie. None of them believed the truth, that he was just a poor white who lived there amongst them because the rent was cheap and he just didn't care about color. To Paul, a man was a man, no matter what his complexion was.

"Thank you, sir," Paul said as he caught the man's eye. "Maybe now I'll be able to get some sleep. Good night, sir, to you and your lady," Paul said, then quickly closed the door.

The man called Jimmy only nodded when he heard Paul speak, but it was enough. Paul was embarrassed. He couldn't figure out why, he only knew that he was. It seemed as if he had been caught listening. He picked up the diary; this was one assured way of getting rid of the feeling. It worked because in moments he was completely absorbed in what he was reading.

Well, it has happened again. But this is the final time. I'll not allow her the chance to ridicule me again. Yes, even as I write this, I am aware my pride has been hurt. It's the main problem; I have too much pride, so I can't accept a woman rejecting me even though I know she cares. But as she says, she happens to be indulging her basic desires. She loves coke but can't afford it, so she uses me.

Do you see, she has done something she should have never done. So sure of her power over me, she came out and made these statements. Juanita might as well have called me a trick. It was the same thing when it was broken down and looked at right. She used me simply because I could afford to pay for all the coke she used. If I didn't have the money, she wouldn't be with me. That's why she laughed whenever I asked her to move in with me. The bitch said she was looking for more out of life than what a petty dope dealer could give her.

Can you dig the nerve of this bitch? She came right out and told me this to my face. I'm what she considers to be a small-time dealer. Well, I've decided to fix her little red wagon for her. At first I asked her if she didn't think it was possible for us to work together and accomplish something. I didn't have to be small-time all my life.

When I told Juanita about this, she burst out laughing. That's right, the dirty whore laughed in my face about it. Then she said that I would be small-time all my life no matter who I had. Again I let my pride get the better of me. I bragged to her that I had ten thousand dollars saved.

Juanita laughed again and said, "See there, that's what I'm talkin' 'bout. You got ten grand saved and think you got some money. Ten thousand dollars ain't shit."

I heard the words she said, while watching her closely. I already knew ten thousand dollars wasn't no money, but I was trying to show her that we had a damn good start. But she didn't give me time to finish before she laughed. But no matter, I still saw the look of greed jump into her eyes. It had surprised her; she hadn't figured I was sittin' on that kind of cash. To take her out, I asked if she wanted to see my bankbook.

The bitch was dying to see it but tried to shine it off. "Hell naw," she drawled coldly, "what you think I am, some kind of freak to get my kicks out of reading what people have in the bank?"

"Well, anyway," I explained, "I just wanted you to know that, if we hooked up together,

134

we wouldn't be coming from the nub. I want to marry you, girl, not just shack up with you."

Her cold laughter killed whatever feelings I'd ever had for her. She thought she was a cold bitch, but she wasn't shit. She had just signed her life over to me. The next time I gave her some cocaine, it was half coke and half heroin. The strongest heroin I could get. Juanita never knew the difference. I began feeding the white poison to her, and in time I'd have my sweet revenge. Don't no bitch laugh in King David's face and never have to pay the price.

Now we began to play at the game which I have come to know so well. In my diary you can see where I have started marking the days. It took three months before the heroin and the cocaine mixed together paid off. After ninety days the bitch was hooked on heroin. Like any other dopefiend in the streets!

11

THE NIGHTCLUB WAS completely silent when Nancy finished singing "I Remember April." Then people inside the club went wild, clapping and stomping their feet. Others in the audience used the knockers that had been passed around.

As though he were the husband of the singer, Moon beamed proudly, his fat face flashing a wide grin for all to see. It made him feel good to know she had left their table and would be coming back as soon as she finished dressing. Her song had been the last one of the night.

The floor show was finished for the evening. People began to get up and leave, some trying to beat the rest of the crowd, while others wanted the company of a group of people going out into the night. In a crowd, there was less chance of getting stuck up in the parking lot.

Alvin watched the people file out. "They remind me of cows, you know what I mean? One following the other."

"What the hell do you know about cows?" Rockie asked, really curious to know where a city boy would find out anything about cows. About the only cows Rockie had seen were those in the movies or on the back of some milk containers.

"When I was doing that bit for the feds, man," Alvin stated, glad to be able to give out some kind of information no one knew anything about, "I worked out at the cow barn. You know, them federal prisons raise their own meat and other shit. Well, it was very interesting."

"Interesting, my ass," Moon said harshly. "Shit, all you did was clean up cow shit. You mean you found that interesting, or was it interesting 'cause you could stick your dick in any cow that was in heat as long as none of the screws caught you."

Rockie broke out laughing. "Goddamn, Alvin, ain't nothing you can say! Ol' Moon is hip to your shit. I'll bet he even got some pictures in his private stash of you pumpin' dick to some sorry-ass cow."

At this statement of his power, Moon roared with laughter. He liked for people to talk about his power. It gave him a good feeling. Even though Moon was what people called a big-time gangster, he still didn't have the power he would like to have. People gave him more credit for strings that he could pull than he really had. Rumors flew around about him, building him as a much bigger man than he really was.

"Hey, Moon," Alvin began, wanting to change the drift of the conversation now, "can you really fix that broad up like you said?"

"What?" Moon yelled, indignant now because his very word was doubted. "Did I hear you say what I thought you said?" Moon's voice dropped back down to a lower tone as he noticed people staring at them.

"Hold on now, Moon," Alvin quickly said, "it ain't like it sounded. I know you can fix up the play so she can cut a record, but I'm talkin' 'bout all that crap you gave her about the gold record. I mean, can you swing some heavy shit like that?"

Alvin knew how to placate his boss. All he had to do was play on the man's immense vanity.

"You're damn right I can! Didn't you hear the goddamn woman sing? It ain't no problem gettin' no gold record. Hell no," he said, speaking more to himself than to his henchmen. "That broad has stardom wrote all over her. I'm just surprised she ain't made it yet." Moon scratched his head slowly. "I mean, you guys heard her; she ain't just started out either, so why in the hell ain't no sharp son-ofabitch picked her up and put her in position to get big money? Talent like what she got ain't easy to find. Shit! Just like the word came to us that there was a dame down here that could really sing, other people have heard it too."

"It do give you reason to think, don't it?" Rockie asked slowly as he began to understand what Moon was saying.

Moon managed to catch Brenda's eye as she

left a party of people she was letting out. She hurried over to the table, wondering what the hell they could want with her now.

"Hey, Brenda," Moon said as she came up, "why don't you square with me? How come a broad as good as Nancy seems to have trouble? She should have been big-time long ago."

Brenda forced her lips into a smile. What the hell, it wasn't no damn secret. Everybody in the business knew about it. "Hell," she began, after glancing around to make sure nobody was listening, "it's not a big secret. You saw her; couldn't you tell?" Brenda waited a second then added, "She drinks, she drinks like a fish. Maybe she has a problem, maybe not. I know she has been slowing down since Mr. Wilson gave her the job here. A few years ago she couldn't hold a job down, but now, well, you have to give her credit, she takes a nip now and then, but she doesn't allow it to come in front of her job."

Moon sat back in his chair and rubbed his chin. "I figured there was somethin' wrong, but since you say she has changed her ways, I'll still take a chance."

Brenda shook her head. "Just don't say anything to her about what I said. Her and I are pretty good friends and I'd like to keep it that way."

"Sure, honey," Moon stated as he pushed his chair back and pulled out his bankroll. He peeled off a twenty-dollar bill and gave it to her. "This is for all the trouble you had to go through for me tonight, Brenda."

She smiled, then tucked the money down in the front of her dress. "Mister Moon," she said as she smiled brightly, "you know it's always a pleasure for me to do business with you." After flashing them another bright smile, she turned and left. It had been a pretty good night after all. Moon had tipped her good and when she added his tips together with the other tips she had received, it was a damn good night for her.

As she walked away, she wished that she could have three or four nights in a row like this one, maybe then she might be able to get that mink coat out of layaway.

Brenda moved to the front of the club, wishing everybody a good night. When she saw Nancy come out, she waved at her and continued to play hostess at the front of the nightclub.

Nancy made her way over to Moon's table. "Well, here I am," she said as she joined them.

"Oh yeah," Moon said as he slowly got to his feet. "Would you care for a drink before we leave?"

Nancy shook her head. "No thank you," she replied quietly. "I'm ready to go whenever you are." Moon had already offered to drop her off. She really wanted to hear more about this wonderful record company he had been talking about.

Moon beckoned to his men and they got up. Rockie and Alvin led the way through the small crowd of people jammed around the front door of the club. For some reason people seemed to like the front of the bar for their last-minute conversations with friends going in another direction.

Brenda was doing her best to shoo them out, but it wasn't enough.

Walking closely behind Alvin and Rockie, Moon and Nancy didn't have much trouble getting through the crowd. The two gunmen just shoved their way through. There were angry yells, but people usually got out of their way after seeing who it was. A few people trying to impress others spoke to Nancy. She waved left and right at people. Some of them were people she really knew, while others were people she had never seen before.

"You're very popular, aren't you?" Moon inquired as he took her arm and propelled her toward the front door. In seconds they were out on the sidewalk. All around them were small clusters of people.

The night air was becoming chilly. Nancy pulled her wrap tighter around her shoulders, but it wasn't really necessary. In a moment they were at the door of the limousine. Rockie held the rear door open for them, while Moon helped Nancy into the backseat. It was the first time Nancy had ever been in such an automobile. As soon as Moon was settled, he reached over and pulled out the bar.

"Well, I'll be damned," Nancy said in surprise. "I've heard about people havin' bars in the back of their car, but this is the first time I've ever seen one with my own eyes."

"Let me fix you a drink, Nancy," Moon said slowly as he began to play bartender.

"Okay," she replied lightly. "Put a touch of lime in it, will you?"

After mixing the drinks, Moon sat back contentedly. He watched the streets flash past. "You know," he began, "this is a wonderful hour to be up. Everybody else is sound asleep, gettin' ready for the morning. But me, I like to be up when daybreak comes. It happens to be a sight that I can never get enough of."

Nancy smiled. "You don't think there will be any problem today over me cuttin' a couple of numbers, do you?" she asked seriously.

Moon let out a deep laugh. "None whatsoever. I've just got to make a call or two in the morning. You have my number, so just do like I say. Call me at one o'clock. By then everything should be set up."

"I hope so," Nancy said seriously. "Every time something looks like it's about to break for me, something that you wouldn't think possible will happen."

"Well, not in this case, dear. You got Moon takin' care of the business end for you, so ain't nothin' going wrong." Moon tossed off his drink and watched the way she toyed with hers. Hell, he reasoned, she damn near had her drinking problem solved. If she was still on the juice, ain't no way she would sit up and nurse that drink.

"You just get you a good night's rest, Nancy," Moon stated like some worried father. "I want you up and ready tomorrow, or rather, today. We are going to have one busy day. First, we have to go by my lawyer's office and sign the contracts. Then we'll end up over at the recording studio."

"I just wish we were on our way there now," Nancy stated nervously. She couldn't get it out of her system. For some reason she was worried. Maybe it just seemed too good to be true. "I mean," she continued, "good things like this just don't happen to me. Something always comes up to spoil them."

Moon laughed loudly. "I tell you, girl, you don't have nothing to worry about." He stared at her closely. "Unless there's something worrying you other than what we have talked about."

The intercom came on and Alvin's voice spoke to them from the front. "We are at her house, boss," he informed them over the speaker.

"Damn!" Nancy said quickly. "I hadn't even noticed, but it's damn sure my apartment building." She turned around and picked up Moon's hand. "Thanks for everything," she said quietly. She fumbled with the doorknob but couldn't get it open.

Suddenly the door opened, but only because Rockie was outside holding the door. She climbed out slowly and flashed them a smile. "Well, I can always say I did get a ride home in style." Alvin closed the door after she got out. They watched her go up the steps, then Alvin got back into the car.

"Where to from here, boss?" Rockie inquired as he glanced back at Moon. The glass partition that had been put up because they had company in the car slowly went down. Now Moon could talk over the seat to his men.

"I don't know. I'm still a littl' bit hungry. Maybe we had better ride down and have us a steak dinner before headin' back to the crib," Moon stated casually. For some reason he wasn't in a hurry to go back home. When he was at the house it was just the other way around, he hated to leave. But once in the streets, he never wanted to rush right back.

"Which steak house should we go to, Moon? You know it's kind of hard to find a good one open," Rockie said, "at this time of night."

"Fuck it!" Moon cursed loudly. "Hell, I don't want just anybody cookin'. It has to be the best." He fell silent for a second, thinking on the problem, then added, "Hell, if I can't get what I want, I don't want a fuckin' thing!"

Moon stared out of the window moodily as the big car moved swiftly through the night. They went through Central Park and came out uptown. Soon they were on Broadway and 54th Street. Turf's Lounge was closed, so they cruised around for a bit, searching for a place that would satisfy Moon's particular tastes.

"I'll tell you what," Moon said as he leaned over and tapped Alvin on the shoulder. "Let's go to the Ham'n'Eggs restaurant. They generally stay open all night and have damn good food."

Alvin parked in front of the restaurant on 51st Street. The three men went in quickly and had a quick meal. When they came back out, they could see streaks of gray in the sky.

"Well, it won't be long now before daybreak," Rockie stated as he held the door open for Moon.

Moon took a quick glance at the sky. "Yeah," he answered slowly, "I guess it's time for us to go in. Maybe I can get a little sleep now." He settled back against the cushions of the car and tried to close his eyes. "Everything has worked out fairly well this evening, so I shouldn't have any complaints. I was lucky enough to swing one of the singingest bitches in the country into my stable. Shit! By the time I get her under a fuckin' contract, why hell, who knows, she just might put out the next number-one record!"

Rockie grinned at his boss. "With your luck, Moon, it shouldn't be too hard."

"Luck, hell," Moon answered sharply. "A man makes his luck. Shit. When I start to make money off this fuckin' songbird, people will say the same thing. Ain't he lucky. But just stop and think for a minute. People been going in there listening to her sing every night, yet nobody has taken advantage of it. I ain't the only person in the world who knows how to go about havin' a goddamn record company cut a record. Shit, all it takes is a little money and enough nerve to take the risk and put up the money.

"But if I get lucky and she does put out a good record, you same niggers will be saying that same cold shit. Ain't Moon lucky!" Moon laughed coldly. "Yeah, I'm lucky, lucky enough to have the brains to know when to put my money out on a good thing. Now drive this fuckin' junk heap on so that I can get me some sleep!"

He looked out at the sky and marveled at how beautiful it was to see dawn breaking, not realizing that it would be the last one he would ever see.

12

———

THE EARLY MORNING hours had slipped away and Paul found himself still awake. He stood up slowly and stretched his long arms over his head. Next he bent down and touched his toes, trying to shake out the cramps he had gotten from sitting in the same position too long.

It was still too early for the morning laborers to be rising. It was that time that you could call the "inbetween" time. The night people were starting to make their way in for the night, while those people with early morning jobs were just reaching over and turning off the alarm clocks.

Paul went into the kitchen and put on a fresh pot of coffee. It was sort of surprising to him to find out that he had consumed a whole pot. Usually, one pot would last two or three days.

As he worked, his mind kept returning to the

diary. King David had been one hell of a man, he reflected, as he waited for the coffee to heat up.

Paul made a useless trip to the icebox, knowing beforehand that there was nothing inside of it that he could eat. He still opened it out of habit and let his eyes roam around the empty shelves. The only thing the refrigerator contained was an old pop bottle that still had a small portion of pop. Paul made a face and closed the refrigerator door.

The sound of the coffee pot steaming came to him suddenly and he knew it was ready. He quickly poured out a cup, then returned to his bed. Lighting up a cigarette first, then setting the ash tray in easy reaching distance, he picked up the diary and settled back to resume his reading.

Janet and her crowd have gone from snorting to shooting dope now. It won't be long before the wheels come off the wagon. I've just about reached one of my goals in the past two years, so money ain't no problem. I ain't never had the kind of money I've got now. I need ten thousand more dollars before I'll have the amount of money I set out to get.

At times I feel as if I should forget about trying to reach fifty thousand dollars, but I'm stubborn as hell. I could freeze right now and never look back. Selling dope is a job. You don't know who to trust, and it's gettin' so bad that your very life is on the line. If things get any worse I might just stop altogether and try something else.

The next entry was dated a week later.

Just came back from Mexico, and I must say, them bitches down there are out of sight. But if you don't speak the language you're in trouble. We went down there to check out a connection, but I don't trust the fuckin' Mexican that I met. I went to nut city on them, 'cause I don't give a fuck. It would be something else if I needed it, but who needs the headache? Not me, that's for damn sure.

The drugs he showed us was supposed to be able to take an eight cut. Now, if I could step on my dope eight times, wow, this nigger would get rich. But that's the hang-up as far as I'm concerned. It's too sweet. Except for the fact that the Mexican won't deliver it across the goddamn border. The honkie I'm partnering up with on this deal still wants to go for it; he believes we can get it out. I'll have to think on the matter a little more. If I could put some faith in the Mexican I just might go for it.

Bill, my partner, still wants to make the buy in Mexico. If we spend four grand apiece, we can get a kilo. Now that is one hell of a deal when you stop and think about it. If we come up with a kilo that we can step on eight times, that will give us eight kilos. Now that's what I would call a hell of an amount of dope. I ain't never had that much stuff on my hands in my life, and I don't think I want it now.

Bill is a user, I just found that out. Even though that doesn't make that much difference it still gives me an insight into why he wants to close this deal so bad. I know it sounds good, but I also realize that if we make the buy we will have to get the drugs out of Mexico, and that's a fuckin' job.

Goddamn, Janet and Bill are bugging the shit out of me to get some cash out so that they can swing this fuckin' deal. Don't know why, but I'm still not sure I want any part of it. For one thing, I don't really need that much stuff. It may sound sort of silly, but I'm afraid to have that much dope around. Shit! If I've made it as far as I've made it without coming close to gettin' busted or ever havin' that much stuff on hand, why the fuck should I change my style of dealing now?

Goddamn, we had a hell of a row when I told Bill and Janet that I wasn't going through with it. Shit, you would have thought that I took their last dollar from them or something. I had to threaten that honkie Bill. Told him I'd step off into his ass if he called me out of my name.

I ain't about to let nobody force me into nothing I don't like. It ain't the money. Hell, if that was the case, I'd give them four grand and let them take all the risks. But that ain't the case. If them goddamn peckerwoods get busted and I got my money tied up with them, shit, the next time I open my door the police would more than likely be there. So I don't want any part of it.

Bill stopped by and told me he was going to cop without me. Just to keep my finger in the pie, I gave him a grand. I did this for insurance. After giving him the grand, I made myself entitled to know his plans. I also told him I didn't want Janet in it. That was my excuse for not gettin' down all the way. He went for it the same way a fly heads for shit!

Janet came over tonight, steaming mad. It seems as if Bill told her what I said. Good. I pulled her coat to the real deal. I don't want her involved. Not because I care for the bitch but because she is the only one in the crowd who knows anything about me. So I don't want anything to happen to her.

Bill and his woman Delores left today for Mexico. They stopped by and I gave them the thousand dollars I'd promised. I also told them to deliver my share of the dope to Janet's pad. I don't want them coming here. Again, this was nothing but the fake-out. As soon as they left, I went back in my bedroom and picked up my suitcases. It just goes to show, I don't trust nobody.

I moved the same day and cut the phone off. I moved to another apartment, one that nobody knows about, not even Janet. This is the best protection I can think of to put on myself. As of now, I don't need it, but you can never tell when you're dealing with addicts and their drugs.

Billy left Monday afternoon for Mexico. Now, three days later, the shit is in the fan. Gerald, the square nigger who stays in the apartment across from the one I moved out of, told me what I had been halfway expecting. I called him this evening. He works days in some kind of factory, but he got the news from his wife when he came home from work.

It seems as if half of Los Angeles' finest detectives raided my old apartment. Now I'm not sure it's related to the trip that Billy made. I can't think of any other mother-fuckin' reason for the police to come storming into where I had lived. From the information that I have been able to gather, the boys in blue were put out because I hadn't sat still and waited for them. If it hadn't been for me using a little foresight, I think I would have been behind bars at this moment, instead of writing these notes down.

Had to post bond to get Janet out of a fuckin' bust that shouldn't have happened. But better her than me. I had my lawyer

Donald Goines

swing the deal because I don't want to get involved. From what I can gather, the police are lookin' for some nigger named King David. Maybe I'll have to change my white slave name and pick me a real soul brother tag. Maybe I'll start calling myself "Mister X." That's as cool as any other.

I lost a thousand dollars on that deal, but I retained my freedom, so it was worth it. Janet wants to suck my ass because I saved her dumb ass from getting busted. If I had allowed her to go along with silly-ass Billy, she would be uptight in Mexico, the same as Billy and his woman.

Now that's tough shit. It still ain't no reason for the bastard to be snitching the way he is. He had to give them Janet's address or they wouldn't have been able to bust her.

It cost me six twenty-five-dollar balloons when they busted Janet. The dumb bitch was layin' up noddin' when they come in on her, so she couldn't clean up. Well, it's her ass, not mine. I'm just glad she didn't have my new address, because they just might have caught me dirty. If not dirty, they would have kept all the cash money they found, or tied it up so that I wouldn't have been able to use it for the next five years.

The white man is a motherfucker. If a nigger has any hopes of ever gettin' ahead, he had better learn how to play the white man's game to only use his own rules. That's the trick, use your own rules. Now I know I've been in Los Angeles about as long as I can last. If I stay here much longer, I'm going to get knocked out of the box.

Even with the setback and the rest of the shit, I gained while losing. Now, I'm only five or six grand away from having my full fifty thousand dollars. I've put in my order for a new Cadillac. It shouldn't be long now.

Paul sat up straight in the bed. Fifty thousand. The thought of the money flashed through his mind. But Paul shook the idea away. Maybe at the time he wrote in the diary he had it, but now, no way. Paul glanced up at the top of the page in the diary. January 10, 1973. Just a few months ago. What could have happened to the money? If what he had been reading in the diary was true, the money should be somewhere around. It had to be. Paul glanced at his hand and noticed he was trembling. Hell, this crap he was reading was bullshit that King David wrote down to pass the time away!

Paul got up and fixed a fresh cup of coffee. He didn't even notice how light it was getting in the room. What the hell, Paul reasoned. If there was any truth in what he read, the diary should give him a key to where the money was. He went back to the bed and reopened the diary. This time his interest was more than just curiosity. Greed was mixed with it.

King David's next entry revealed the foresight the man had had.

Since moving, Janet has no way of gettin' in touch with me. That's cool, 'cause I know the cops are watching her. I rapped with her on the phone but got tired of listening to the bitch beg. She's supposed to be sick. Tough shit. It ain't my problem if she was silly enough to let herself get strung out.

This crazy bitch had the nerve to tell me that it was my fault that she was a junkie. It's hard to believe, but that's what she says. Well, I do feel sort of responsible for her, so I left her a small package at the motel where I first met her. Yes, it just goes to show that I've really got a heart. She doesn't know it yet but that was the last time we will ever do anything together. So it was sort of a going-away package from me.

I left her a piece of stuff. It's worth over five hundred dollars, so if Janet uses any kind of sense, she should be able to get herself together with it. Shit, ain't nobody ever did nothing like that for me, just up and gave me somethin'. Shit! No way!

Now I have got problems. Juanita is acting up. I had hoped to do something for the bitch, like break both her legs before I left or something like that. I got her strung out damn good, and I know she's been turning tricks to keep up her habit, but that ain't enough for me. I want to see that dirty bitch wallow in mud before I leave, but it don't look like I'm going to get the chance to see it.

I might as well put the truth down, since I'm the only one who will ever see this while I'm living. I got weak at the last moment. Yes, I still found myself drawn to the dirty bitch even though she had damn near spit on me. Well, I offered her a chance again, even though I knew she was a junkie. Now can you imagine a dopefiend-ass bitch turning down a sure thing? I told her I'd help her with her habit. But instead of that making her happy she screamed on me.

"Help me?" she screamed. "I'd rather have help from a snake! If it wasn't for you, you bastard, I wouldn't be in the shape I'm in now."

Well, from her words, it wasn't hard for me to figure out that she was hip to the fact that I had handed her heroin for coke until she was strung out. But still, it was too much when she cursed at me.

"King David, you lowlife motherfucker you! If it were any way possible, I'd see to it that the police jammed your ass in jail and kept you there until the fuckin' walls fell down!"

Yeah, I think those are just about her correct words. Even when I write them down I get that cold feeling that practically strangled me the day she tossed them in my face.

When she talked about police, I knew the bitch was dangerous, but I still wouldn't have wasted any time on her. I didn't think there was anything she could pin on me.

I can still remember the day she called crying and told me she was sick, but it wouldn't be for long. If she could only get a favor that morning she would be all right, because she had called the Bricks Foundation and they were going to send somebody over to pick her up. Yeah, the bitch was going in the hospital to kick. She was planning on getting the monkey off her back once and for all.

It was as if someone had tossed cold water in my face. Kick! If the whore ever kicked, she would be back where she began. I knew I couldn't have that. I had to make the funky black bitch pay for her arrogant ways. Ain't a bitch alive ever treated me the way she had, and now she was planning on kicking the habit.

The only thing that I had on her was the knowledge that I had strung her out, and I knew that as long as she remained a junkie she would catch pure hell.

So I made my plans accordingly. Since she was committing herself that afternoon, it didn't leave much time. I was supposed to be picking up my new ride that morning too, so I went into the bedroom and started to pack. As I stacked the fifty grand neatly in my bag I made my final plans for her.

Paul reread the sentence about the money, then leaped up from the bed and ran to the closet where he had shoved the other small suitcases without opening them. He carried a bag back to the bed and tried to open it but found a small lock on it. He didn't bother to check the keys on the key ring. He just took a small knife and forced the lock.

The clothes stacked neatly on top were shoved to the side. As soon as he moved them Paul saw the first bundle of money. He held his breath and then started to take them out one at a time. For a long time afterward, Paul just sat on the edge of the bed and stared at the money. It was the first time he had ever seen so much of it. He didn't even bother to count it. If King David said there was fifty thousand dollars there, he believed it was more.

Fifty thousand dollars! Paul had trouble getting over the shock of it. Then his mind went back to what he had been reading and he wondered about what had happened to the girl. She had caught so much hell already just for having been unlucky enough to have met King David. For him to be crazy enough to have done something to her was too much for Paul to believe. King David had to have been mad, Paul believed. The man had surely been insane. Paul stacked the money back like he found it, then pushed the suitcase under the bed. Then he reopened the diary.

Since I don't have much time, I've decided to make my moves all at one time. The dope that I had left I fixed up into another package and put it between a folded newspaper. I called Janet and told her I had another package for her and where she could pick it up.

The next thing I did was to pick up the small package of raw dope that I had and fixed it up for Juanita. Since it was pure, I didn't worry about it too much. But just so that I wouldn't take any chances I made a trip down to my old Caddie and opened the hood up and scraped some of the white battery acid off the battery. I took this back upstairs to my apartment and reopened the small package of dope. I shook the acid out and mixed it up until I couldn't even tell the difference between it and the pure dope.

To make sure everything was going to go right, I called Juanita up and told her I'd bring her some stuff but she had to be by herself. Being so self-centered, the bitch instantly thought that I wanted to bed her down and, like a true dopefiend, came up with a story instantly.

"I'm on my period, David," she said, lying through her motherfuckin' teeth.

"Yeah," I answered, "but ain't nothing wrong with your head, is it?" I was just playing along, letting her silly ass think I really wanted her.

To cap it off, I asked her was she sure she wanted some stuff, since she was going in the hospital that day. I played my cards to a tee. Knowing dopefiends the way that I did, I knew she couldn't turn down that last fix. None of them can, not while they are still strung out.

She tried to fight it. For a minute I thought I might have over-spotted my hand, mentioning the hospital to her. Since she had made up her mind to go in the hospital I knew she was tired of using, but the attraction of the drug won out.

"Okay, David," she answered in a weak voice, "I'll be here. You're not going to be too long, are you?" she asked, in that lost little girl voice she sometimes used.

"Don't worry about a thing, momma," I answered, then hung up. I checked the small package out once more, then I took all my bags downstairs and put them in the car. After that, I went back upstairs and wiped everything off, hoping that I didn't leave any prints. Though there was really no reason for this. I did it anyway, being on the safe side and all that shit.

It took me a few minutes to drive the freeway, then I was parking a few doors down from her house. Again there was no reason for me to be careful since I was trading the old Cadillac in on a new model in another hour, but I used caution anyway. Practice makes perfect, so they say. So I was careful.

Juanita was waiting at the top of the stairs for me. She led me back to her apartment. I checked, making sure nobody saw me as I entered her room. She didn't waste any time. She had her cooker ready, but I put her off.

"Hey baby," I yelled, "ain't you forgettin' something?"

She wet her lips. "We can take care of that after I get the stuff in me, King. I'm sick right now."

"Sick, my ass," I screamed on her. "I don't want no dead head," I said, then burst out laughing. She couldn't dig what was so funny, but I did. Dead head. That's just what it would have been. "Naw, baby," I stated coldly, then walked over to the couch and flopped down on it. I opened up my pants and pulled out my jones and let it hang down. "You better get a towel or something. I don't want spit all over me."

There were real tears in her eyes as she turned away from me. I knew she wanted to tell me to kiss her ass, but she didn't have the nerve. She wanted the dope too badly.

She went to the bathroom and got the towel. I made her kneel down in front of me, then I rubbed my dick all over her face until it was covered with her tears. I wanted to fuck her then real bad. As she started to sob, I pushed her away, and fell down on the floor next to her. She was crying loudly now. The sounds of her shame only aroused me.

"Hey, momma, you ain't forgot me, have you?" I inquired coldly. "This is the little man, remember? The one who would never be nothing, or something like that. What was it?" I asked, as I forced her legs wider. She didn't have any Kotex inside, so I was right. The bitch had lied.

I could feel the soft hairs over her crack and they aroused me like always. It was at this time that she reminded me of a white girl. She was the first black girl I'd ever bedded who had soft hairs on her crack. I rammed my dick up in her, making her grunt from the pain. I'm pretty well hung, so I can get a sound or two out of the average woman.

With her legs spread as far as I could get them, I started to ride that pussy. She cried like a baby, causing me to bust my nuts before I was ready to come. I wanted to have another nut, but she wasn't about to stand still for it. She wanted to shoot the dope at once. There was nothing I could do to prevent it.

I went into the bathroom and washed up, making sure I didn't leave any prints. When I came out she had the dope cooked up and was searching for a vein. I started to leave. There was no reason for me to watch it. But she got a hit before I could get out the door.

Her eyes were large as she watched me, then they carried a look of surprise.

Her mouth opened as if she wanted to scream, but no sound came. She rubbed wildly at her arm as she snatched the outfit out, then fell over onto her side. She kicked once or twice, then she was perfectly still. I walked over and looked down at her. Snot poured from her nose and a long stream of it fell down on her chin. Her legs were wet from where her bowels had busted on her.

As I stared down at her, a lump of shit came running down her leg. I looked at it and the thought flashed through my mind that she wasn't so fuckin' fine after all.

After one more glance at Miss Fine-and-Mighty, I turned on my heel and departed, on my way to pick up my new Cadillac. And then from there, I'd hit the highway. Like I said, Los Angeles and me had had enough of each other. It was time for me to go back to the Big Apple.

After all, I've been out here for damn near five years. It's time I slowed down. Maybe now I can settle down and live respectably. Something I've been wanting to do all my life.

13

"THAT'S A BEAUTIFUL sight, boys," Moon said, drawing the other two men's attention to the sky. "Look at it. Ain't no artist living can capture that beauty on canvas. No sirree, that's something can't nothin' touch."

"Hell, Moon, I ain't never figured you for a nature lover," Alvin said with a grin. "Now me, I don't never notice nothing until I get locked up. Then I can see a bird flyin', and I'll watch it fly. Or wonder about a fuckin' mouse and figure he better off than me. Yeah, that goddamn jailhouse will make a man notice everything."

"Shit," Rockie said, not wanting to be left out, "I was raised on a farm. What I miss is that country smell, you know? The grass smellin' fresh and the wind blowing, without the smell of factories in the air. Now that's somethin' ain't nobody able to put together. The real fresh air of the country."

"What you miss about the country," Moon said with that cold wit of his, "is the outhouses and wipin' your ass with your thumb 'cause you poor-ass country boys sure in hell can't afford to buy no goddamn toilet paper!"

All the men laughed loudly at the truth of the statement. Rockie grinned sheepishly. "Hell, Moon," he answered, "we didn't have to use our thumb. Hell, any old country boy will tell you all you need is some of that sweet-smellin' grass. Shucks, boss, it's even better than some of this paper you buy up in Harlem."

"Yeah?" Moon answered sarcastically. "If it is, you better change the store you're shoppin' at!" Moon grunted as he leaned over and began to fix himself another drink. "Either one of you boys want me to fix you somethin'? I don't usually play bartender, but I'll break down this time and play Santa."

"Yeah," Alvin said quickly, "I'll have one, boss. How 'bout a shot of scotch with a dab of milk if you got any." He knew all the time there was milk back there because he stocked the bar.

"Make mine the same thing, only keep the milk out of it," Rockie stated.

Moon mixed the drinks expertly, then passed them over the seat. "You boys hurry up and drink them down. We don't want no hassle from no cop if we should be unlucky enough to be stopped by them." Moon drained off his drink, then fixed another one. He closed his eyes and nursed the drink in his lap. At this rate, I'll end up being a fuckin' rummy, he warned himself.

Rockie handed the glasses back over the seat as soon as they finished them. "Thanks, boss," he said, smacking his lips to show his appreciation. "It ain't every day a nigger like me gets a chance to drink whiskey like this."

"Rockie," Moon said, "you're a goddamn liar. You get a chance to drink good whiskey every day, 'cause whenever you think I ain't lookin' you fix a quick one off my bar!" Moon glanced at his watch. "I'll be glad to reach the pad. I feel like I can sleep the rest of the week. Boys, we goin' have to start going out more. I really enjoyed myself tonight. Hell, I need to get out. Maybe it will help me stop drinkin' so much. You know, just hangin' around the apartment a man ain't got nothing else to do but take a drink to kill the time. That's our problem, too much fuckin' time on our hands. Maybe I'll start going out to the track." Moon's voice had dropped to a whisper as the hard liquor hit him.

Alvin glanced in the mirror and shook his head. He sometimes wondered how much liquor Moon could hold without falling out. The man seemed to be bottomless. Whiskey didn't affect Moon the way it did other men. He never seemed to get drunk. The only thing it seemed to do to him was make him sleepy.

As the long automobile weaved its way through the light morning traffic, another figure waited patiently for its arrival. Mike walked to the corner, then turned around and came back past the apartment building. His steps grew slower as he came abreast of the entrance, then he continued on. For a minute he hesitated, undecided on whether or not he should go on up.

Maybe Moon was upstairs. Maybe he just sent the big car out to be fixed or something. It wasn't like Moon to stay out all night, so maybe he wasn't out at all. That would be a bitch if Moon was upstairs and had been up there all this time.

Mike leaned against the wall. His wounds were acting up. He had lost too much blood. If he continued on like he was doing, he wouldn't have the strength to do the job when the chance arose.

Finally, out of desperation, Mike decided to go upstairs and find out for himself. This waiting was too much. He glanced up at the sky. No, it didn't make sense. Moon didn't stay out this late. He couldn't think of anywhere that Moon could be this late. More than likely he was upstairs in his bed, sleeping like he owned the world.

Straightening up, Mike pushed himself away from the wall. He made sure he had himself under control before starting toward the entrance. He didn't want to draw too much attention to himself, so he walked carefully, taking measured steps. The lights inside the lobby almost blinded him. He blinked once or twice, then made his way toward the elevator.

Mike wasn't worried about being noticed because he knew the night man on the desk was aware he worked for Moon. There wouldn't be any unwanted questions. But he was lucky anyway, because the desk clerk had left his station for a minute, and the bellboy on night duty was dozing in a chair.

Mike took his time and tiptoed across the large well-furnished lobby. He stepped into the waiting elevator and pushed the button that would take him to the top floor. The elevator went up without making any noise and stopped on the penthouse floor.

Mike walked down to the apartment, then stopped at the door. He checked the pistol in his belt, removed it, and placed it in his coat pocket where he could keep his hand on it. If necessary, he would be able to shoot through his coat.

Mike rang the bell with three short bursts—the signal that only members of the gang knew about. Jo-Jo, the Japanese houseboy, opened the door. He stared at Mike. "You no with boss tonight?" he asked. Mike brushed on past him into the apartment.

"Hell no," Mike answered. "Where the hell is Moon?"

Not really knowing, Jo-Jo shook his head. "Me not know. Boss no tell me he gone. He no tell me nothing."

"Okay, Jo-Jo," Mike said. "You can go to bed. I'll be here when Moon comes back, so don't you worry about it."

"Good, good," Jo-Jo replied with a short bow, then disappeared into the rear of the apartment, where the bedrooms were located.

Mike began to feel weak. He stumbled toward the bathroom. Once inside he pulled his shirt loose and looked at the wounds. He didn't know anything about stopping a cut from bleeding. The only thing he could think of was to wet a wash-cloth and hold it against the wound.

172

Soon, the heat from the cloth soothed him to such a degree that he found himself nodding on his feet. His head would fall forward for a while, then suddenly he would wake up. He sat down on the toilet seat, his head nodding against his chest.

Mike was in that position when Moon and his two gunmen came in. They walked into the apartment and stopped at the bar. Mike was asleep in the bathroom and didn't even wake up.

Rockie went behind the bar and poured himself a drink. "You want one before turning in, boss?"

"Yeah," Moon answered loudly. "I might as well. It helps me to sleep better at night." Rockie filled the two drinks and looked at Alvin, who declined. Alvin then pushed past Rockie and opened the panel.

"You want your pistol out of here, Rockie?" he inquired as he took his own gun down.

"Naw, I'll get it a little later on. Shit, it felt good not havin' that weight on me for a change," Rockie said as he finished mixing the drinks and pushed Moon's double shot toward him.

"Well, I felt naked myself," Alvin replied and stuck his gun in his waistband.

Moon and Rockie toasted each other, knocking

their glasses together. The sounds of their voices finally reached Mike in the toilet. He listened for a brief second, then removed his pistol from his coat pocket and started toward the door.

He hesitated for a moment, then quietly pushed the bathroom door open and stepped into the living room. The three men didn't see him until he was almost upon them. It wasn't until Alvin saw the gun in Mike's hand that he realized they were in danger.

At the look on Alvin's face, Moon spun around on his barstool. One glance at Mike coming toward them caused Moon's bowels to become loose. The look on the man's face didn't leave any questions. There was murder in his eyes.

Moon let out a scream of pure panic and tried to run around the bar. The first shot from Mike's gun took him right between the shoulderblades. A second shot shattered his spine. As he slumped forward, knocking a tray of glasses down, Rockie rushed toward the panel. He managed to push the button, but the sliding door was too slow.

Mike's next shot took Rockie in the forehead, knocking him backward against the panel. Before Mike could fire again, Alvin had squeezed off two shots, both of them taking Mike high in the chest. He bounced back off the wall and tried to raise his pistol again, but another bullet smashed into his mouth and he was dead before he hit the floor.

14

PAUL SLOWLY PUT the diary down. Now he knew everything except why King David was killed. It didn't really matter now, though. After what he had just read he knew that the man needed killing. He shouldn't have been allowed to live.

Now it was up to Paul to bury him. The very thought of it was repugnant. But he had given his word. He really didn't have to do anything but make the arrangements and then forget about it. But the more he thought about it, the more he decided not to waste too much money on the funeral.

Paul slowly dressed. It would have been nice to be able to take the money and go into one of the big men's stores downtown and buy what he wanted, but he didn't believe he could ever wear the clothes in peace. After he got dressed, he picked up the small suitcase that he had put the money into and started for the door.

His first stop was a mortuary where he made arrangements to have the body cremated. It was cheaper that way.

After he left the funeral home, he drove around slowly, searching for just the right place. Down by 137th Street he found just what he was looking for. It was a drug center that worked with youths from the city.

Paul walked inside and glanced around casually. It was his first time inside such a place. He asked the young girl at the desk for the supervisor, then he sat down and waited for about ten minutes until a brown-skinned woman came out of a rear office and walked toward him. Paul introduced himself, then she led the way back to her office.

The sign on her desk read "Mrs. Johnson."

"Mrs. Johnson," Paul began, "I don't want to take up too much of your time. . . ."

But she cut him off. "Oh, don't worry about it; that's what we are here for, sir, to help people." She smiled at him openly, and he was sure he had come to the right place.

"You do work with drug addicts, don't you?" Paul inquired seriously.

"Of course. That was one of our reformed girls out there at the desk," Mrs. Johnson said.

"Good, good," Paul replied. "I have something for you. The only thing I want to be sure of is that you really use it on the drug addicts. Help them to help themselves. I don't care if you give the money to them or buy whatever you think they need."

At the mention of money her eyebrows went up. "Money," she said in surprise. "I don't think I understand you, sir."

Paul smiled at her, then set the bag on top of her desk. He flipped it over and the bundles of money came tumbling out. "This is for your people. Use it as you see fit." Paul got up and walked out of the stunned woman's office.

Mrs. Johnson stared at the strange man as he walked away. She didn't speak. She was afraid he would return and pick up the money.

Mrs. Johnson didn't spend the money right away. She held it for just over a month before spending the first dollar, just in case he had come back for it.

After Paul left, he got into the Cadillac. "Well," he said aloud, "I guess I'll keep the car. That much I do owe myself." He smiled, then thought about the funeral arrangements. Yes, it was the best thing he could have done. Why waste money on expensive funerals when the same money could be used to help some of the people King David had used to get the large sum of money.

The junkies who were still alive were damn sure more in need of it than King David and his kind would ever be!

Keep reading for a special preview
of Donald Goines's

BLACK GANGSTER

1

THE SUN WAS SHINING through the bars on the window as Prince, tall, slim, and black, got up from his bed and paced back and forth in his cell. He stopped in front of the small calendar he kept on the wall and smiled. It had been a long time but he had managed to keep his sanity. Suddenly the sound he had been waiting for reached him loud and clear.

"Break one!" The yell was sharp and, before it had diminished, the sound of over a hundred steel doors opening together drowned it out. "Break two!" came the yell again, followed by another hundred iron doors opening at the same time. Voices were raised in harsh humor as over four hundred men joked and argued back and forth. "Break three," the break man screamed as he reached the third gallery.

Prince glanced into the small mirror hanging

over his facebowl, reached up and patted down his large afro hairstyle and then rushed to the front of his cell and snatched open the steel door. Then he stepped out on the gallery, slamming the door behind him with the experience of a convict who has been jailing for a long time. He quickly glanced back into his cell to see whether his bed was wrinkled. It was more a reflex motion than any real concern for the appearance of his cell.

Prince fell in step with the man in front of him. "How you feel, baby, gettin' up this morning?" the white inmate who locked next to him asked. From the sound of the man's voice, there was no way of telling whether he was black or white. This was not unusual in prison. Many white men after spending a lot of time behind prison walls adopted the mannerisms of black men.

"What's happening, Red?" Prince replied easily as they started down the concrete stairs. Glancing down from the third-floor gallery all you could see was a line of blue-dressed men.

"Break four!" came the yell as the break man let out the men locking on the fourth gallery. The sound of a hundred steel doors slamming shut came to their ears as they hurried down the stairway.

"Stop that running down there," a guard yelled from his gun tower. The gun tower was up on the fourth floor, built down from the ceiling, away from the gallery. The only way a man could reach it was from the roof. A prisoner could spend a lifetime behind the walls and never come close to seeing the inside of a gun tower. All he would ever see would be the bright steel of the gun barrel sticking out of one of the many slots.

The inmate guilty of running slowed down after he reached the friend he had run to catch up with. They began talking loudly as they continued on towards the line of men lined up on the base, the bottom floor. The sound of so many voices talking together was like the hum of a million bees. The old silent system had been abolished many years before. Now inmates could talk on the way to chow, while sitting in the dining hall, even while standing in the line as they went to eat. Jackson Prison, the largest penal institution in the United States, was becoming modern.

The men lined up and the guards waited patiently until the men quieted down before opening the doors and allowing them to file out quietly. Guards walked up and down the line speaking to individual prisoners.

"What's wrong, Jones, you ain't hungry this morning? You there, Collins, keep the bullshit up; we got all fuckin' day. If you don't eat, it's your own damn fault." From close association, most of the guards spoke the same language the inmates used. "I guess don't none of these boys want to peck today," the sergeant said loudly. He rubbed his huge potgut and laughed. None of the guards working the floors, or blocks, or yard, were allowed to carry any form of weapon. There were no more nightsticks or guns at the guards' sides. If violence occurred, it was up to the guard to get his ass to cover or under one of the gun towers.

The line of men soon quieted down enough to satisfy the guards. They started filing out the large doors of Three Block. The other eight blocks inside the prison walls had already eaten.

Prince walked beside Red, shooting the bull until they reached the mess hall. Then, by tacit agreement, the men split up, blacks going in one side of the huge mess hall, whites in the other side. The men segregated themselves in the mess hall by personal choice, blacks eating on one side, whites on the other. Here and there you could see a sprinkling of whites sitting with blacks. In most of these instances it was a white homosexual sitting with his man, or when it occurred on the white side, a black homosexual sitting with his white man. At times, it would just be friends sitting together, but it was more than likely to be lovers together.

At all times during the meal, the men were kept under surveillance by the men in the gun towers. At the first sign of any disturbance, long-barreled rifles would appear in the gun slots. It was a known fact amongst the inmates that the guards would shoot, and shoot quick. It didn't take much to give them cause for target practice. In prison, a man quickly learned that, at the beginning of any fight, you got the hell clear of the fighting area, because when the guards started to fire, it would be right into the crowd of fighters.

Donald Goines

Prince ate quickly and left the mess hall. It was yard time now, so he had a few hours until it started to get dark before locking back up. He searched through the gym first, looking for his older friend, Fox. The gym was full of men playing basketball on the two courts, plus men in the weight pits, lifting iron over their heads, trying to build muscles up so they could impress their girl-friends when they got out. On the benches lining the walls men sat huddled over, playing chess and checkers, cigarettes stacked up beside them to bet with.

Prince retraced his steps and walked over to "Las Vegas," a large area with wooden tables and seats. Here the men gambled from the beginning of yard time until it ended, winter or summer. In the winter you could find them huddled up in their coats, betting boxes of cigarettes as if they were real money. To them, they were money; in prison, cigarettes take the place of currency. You could buy everything from a homemade knife to a sex act with one of the many queers who lived like beauty queens inside the prison walls. All it took was cigarettes. To have a quick relationship with one of the younger, prettier queers, it would cost two cartons of smokes, any brand. Older ho-mosexuals would sell themselves for five packs on up. The prices varied with the merchandise; any sissy, no matter how ugly he might be, could find a boyfriend. From eighteen up to eighty, if they had a hot head or whatever else it took, somebody inside the prison walls would gladly become his man.

Fox saw Prince coming and stepped away from the poker game he had been watching. "Hey there, guy, I been lookin' for you."

"Yeah, Fox, the bastards fed us last today," Prince said as he walked up to his associate. Fox was in his late thirties, with the appearance of a man in his early fifties. His eyes had deep circles around them, while there was a thinning out of his hair that came with old age. His face was slightly bloated, and his pale brown skin had a burned look about it, as though it had seen too much scorching sun. He was short, about five-seven, with a growing paunch. His gut hung over his belt buckle.

"Let's walk around awhile." His voice was firm and strong.

Prince fell in step with the older man. He had grown accustomed to Fox's way of speaking long ago. He was not necessarily used to people talking to him in this manner, but he had long ago learned to accept certain things if he thought that they would one day pay off in his favor.

They walked side by side around the yard. As they passed the stands Prince waved to Red, who was sitting with some hillbillies playing guitars.

"Goddamn, it's more fuckin' woods with guitars inside this joint than it's roaches in the city," Fox said and removed his hankie to wipe sweat from his brow. "The goddamn hot weather brings them out with them funky guitars like flies."

Prince laughed and continued to walk without comment. He was used to hearing Fox curse over just about everything inside the prison. Fox had done nine years on a twenty-year sentence for sale of heroin. He would be going up for a special in another month, and with his good record Prince was hoping that he made it. With the release of Fox, his plans would be falling right in order. He needed that good connect that Fox had with the dagos. A good heroin connect with Italians would make a young, fast black man rich.

"Hey, Prince, you got a minute?" an elderly black man called.

Both men stopped and waited for the older man to catch up. "I just wanted to find out if you could let me have a couple of packs, Prince. I got some good spud-juice lined up, but it takes five packs to cop."

"I'm sorry, Dad. I done gave away all my extra stuff," Prince answered politely, smiling and revealing evenly spaced white teeth.

The old man shook his head and walked away. "I should have remembered you're gettin' up in the morning," he answered over his shoulder.

"I just can't understand why you waste your time fuckin' with them deadbeats, Prince," Fox said as he coldly watched the older man walk away.

"He wasn't always down and out, man. He's just gettin' old now, and times done passed him by," Prince answered, then added, "I remember him from the old neighborhood, Fox. He used to always have time for us kids when he was doing good. He'd pull up in that white Caddie he drove, and we'd always be able to hit him up for a few dollars."

"He was a goddamn fool," Fox said harshly. "When he caught his case, that nigger had big money. More than the average nigger ever sees in a lifetime. Now look at him. Anytime a old man's fool enough to leave all his money with a young bitch, he's supposed to get took."

That was true enough, Prince agreed silently. He had the same thoughts. Not only any old man, but any young one, too. Still, it didn't stop him from being kind to the old man. He believed kindness was the sweetest con of all. Ever since he had been here, he had used a pleasant front, picking the men around him so subtly that they never knew he was using them. It had taken him two weeks to pick the little knowledge out of old Dad. Now he knew how old Dad had gotten rich, which people he had gone to to get the connections he needed to get his whiskey stills made. All of this and more was written down in his cell.

He knew just the people to go to for sugar connects, where he could buy twenty thousand pounds of sugar without any static. In fact, when his woman had come up to visit him last month, he had had her check it out, and now it was all set up, ready for him to get it out and put the business into operation. He smiled silently as he remembered her last letter. She had mentioned that she had a hundred thousand pounds of sweetness for him whenever he got out. The guards who censored the mail would have never realized that she was talking about sugar stashed away in an empty slum house.

"I don't know how that old bastard made the kind of money he was supposed to have made off of corn whiskey anyway," Fox said as they started to walk again. "It ain't that kind of money in no whiskey, in this day and age. This is the sixties, not the roaring twenties."

You know-all bastard, you, Prince thought coldly. Just continue thinking that way. "Maybe you're right at that, Fox," he said, agreeing with him as he always did whenever he knew there was no point in starting a useless argument.

There was a crowd in the middle of the yard, so they stopped and watched it for a few moments. Two men stood closely together, while another man stood in front of them with a bible. It was just another marriage going on. Almost weekly in the large prison, some homosexual was getting married to another man behind the bleak walls of the prison. It had become so regular that few people stopped to watch it.

"Goddamn punks!" Fox cursed loudly, his words carrying to the men in the rear of the crowd.

"Hey, Prince," one of the men yelled from the crowd. "They passing out ice cream and pop as soon as the wedding is over."

"That's all right, Bull. I got some script. We might stop at the store on the way around and pick up something," Prince replied with humor.

"Unless you want some of their cream," he said to his companion.

"I'd rather be dead first," Fox replied with his usual impoliteness. "You know me better than that, Prince. That shit is for these goddamn parasites like Bull. Whenever you hear of something being given away, you'll find him in the front of the fuckin' line. I wish they would give away some shit sandwiches. He'd probably be right down front for that, too."

Prince glanced down at his companion. Again he wondered how the man had survived nine years behind the walls without getting himself killed. Fox bitched about anything and everything. If he wasn't crying over the food, he was complaining about the lousy movies that came inside the prison once a week.

"About that favor I been asking you about, Fox. You goin' do that for me?"

"I don't know, Prince. I gave it a lot of thought, man, but it just ain't right. I can't send you to them people like that." Before Prince could interrupt, he continued. "You just wait until I get out, baby, and we'll go over to the Big Apple together."

Prince remained silent for a minute. It was no more than he had thought would happen. He had never really believed that Fox would give him the connection in New York, but he had kept on trying until his last day in prison.

"Yeah, man, yeah. I didn't believe you'd act like a true friend, Fox," he said, some of his anger displayed in his voice. "After fuckin' around with me for over three years, Fox, you still don't trust me enough to let me get this thing off the ground for us. By the time you get out, man, I could be done made fifty grand."

"Hold on there, Prince, just hold on. Look here. When I go to the board, if I don't make it, I'll write and let you know. Then all you got to do is send your woman up to see me and I'll give her the information you need."

"Sure, baby, sure," Prince answered and turned his back and walked away. If it happened, cool, but if it didn't, he had other irons in the fire. By this time next year, he planned to have the city of Detroit wrapped up. It wasn't a bad dream for a young man of twenty-two. He had come to prison at the tender age of eighteen; now, four years later, he was educated with a schooling that a man could get nowhere else but in prison. He had learned the hard way that, if you were going to live a life of crime, go for the big buck. Now he was ready.

2

THE GREYHOUND BUS roared through the out-skirts of Detroit. Prince twisted around in his seat and pretended to stare out of the window. He tried to ignore the slim, blond man next to him. They had both been released from the prison at the same time that morning. After reaching the bus station they had been left alone, but for some reason the young white man hadn't wanted it that way. He continued to stay close to Prince. When the bus arrived, he had followed Prince to the back of the coach and sat beside him. Prince stretched out his long legs as a bell went off in the back of his mind. "No, it couldn't be," he told himself and tried to push the thought out of his head. After leaving queers alone for four years while in prison, it couldn't be possible for one to try to pick him up on his first day out. He went back over their conversation slowly, looking for a hint of the truth. For the first few minutes of the ride, they had talked about the prison, then they both had started speaking about their futures. After a few minutes of this, Prince attempted to change the conversation back to prison. He had quickly grown tired of talking about choppers. After twenty minutes of being told how to turn some kind of 1957 motorcycle into a chopper, he turned his back on the boy in disgust.

Here was a sonofabitch twenty-five years old, he thought, who believed all you had to do was get a fuckin' motorcycle and you had it made with all the bitches in the world. This bastard is queer as a three-dollar bill, Prince told himself coldly as his eyes turned a frosty gray. All this crap about motorcycles is a fake-out. He listened to the young man's voice go on and on until he finally decided to put an end to it.

Prince turned back around and stared the young man in the eyes. "How would you like to go to a motel when we get in the city?" Prince asked sharply.

Now that it was out in the open, Prince could see the man's desire. His hesitation was only a fake-out. "What? I mean, I don't do those kind of things," the young man replied uneasily. He was nervous, and his hands shook slightly as he lit a cigarette.

"Don't give me that shit," Prince answered harshly. "You been had before. I been trying to place you ever since we left the joint, and now I got you pegged. You used to be Eddie Townsend's woman in the joint. Don't bullshit me, 'cause it won't do you any good."

The young man shook his head. "That's not true," he said. "You really must have me mixed up with someone else."

"Bullshit!" Prince answered coldly. "What did you say your name was? Johnnie. Yeah, that's right. They used to call you Johnnie-may. I remember your little fine ass now."

Johnnie dropped his head, too frightened or ashamed to speak. He dropped his eyes, afraid to return Prince's stare.

Now that Prince had hit on the right track, he continued more ruthless than he needed to be. He wanted to browbeat the kid. "You know you been had, Johnnie boy, ain't you? So why you want to start acting like a man now? You didn't act like one while you was in the joint, did you?" He laughed harshly, the sound of his laughter filling the coach.

The young man's eyes searched Prince's face with desperation. He muttered brokenly, "They made me do it. They made me, I swear to God, they forced me to."

Beginning to tire of his little game, Prince said flatly, "I knew there wasn't no way for no fine young blond bitch like you to go behind the walls and come out without being touched up." His words beat at Johnnie like a tattoo. "Why did you come on with all that motorcycle crap when you sat down here anyway, boy? Was that your way of making me think you're bad or something?" Prince shook his head. "Well anyway, boy, you ain't got to worry about me. I don't use. I don't care if you're a punk or not. It don't make me any difference one way or the other."

Prince didn't even glance around when Johnnie got up and walked to the front of the coach. He bent down and spoke softly to the driver. At the next red light the driver pulled over. With his small shoe box clutched under his arm, Johnnie jumped from the bus.

Prince watched him depart, carrying the accumulation of junk that he had collected while in prison. As the bus pulled away, Johnnie started to wave, then caught himself and looked away. Prince smiled to himself as he stared at his own reflection in the window. His heavy eyebrows seemed to meet as he scowled out at the passing scenery.

In a few minutes the bus was parking in the terminal. Prince grabbed up his few belongings and pushed his way to the front. One woman complained loudly as he pushed his way between her and her children. He glanced back over his shoulder and caught her with an icicle glare. For years he had waited and thought of the day when he would return home. In none of his wildest dreams had he imagined being cursed out by some woman on his first day out. For a brief moment, some of the ruthlessness he kept concealed beneath a front of good humor revealed itself.

The woman glanced away from him quickly and busied herself with her four children. As she bent down to straighten out one of her kids' jackets, Prince got a glimpse of a full black bosom and his anger left. It had been years since he had seen anything close to a woman's breasts, and the sight was rewarding enough to restore his anticipation. He continued on his way, elbowing a fat salesman out of his path as he hurried down the steps of the bus.

Once free from the pushing of the crowd of departing passengers, Prince stopped and allowed himself to breathe deeply, enjoying the taste of freedom. He stared around as if it were his first time in a big city. Any passerby would have taken him for a country boy on his first trip to a large city. His face lit up with a broad smile as he stared around at the milling crowd of people. His happiness was easy to see.

Suddenly he spotted a group of teenagers standing off to the side. People seemed to be giving them a lot of room. He waved and started to make his way in their direction. The leader of the group was standing out in front of them, posing, and scrutinizing the passengers with as much disgust in his stare as he could possibly manage.

A look of recognition appeared in Roman's eyes as he noticed Prince breaking through the crowd. "Over here, baby," he yelled loudly. The gang rushed forward to meet Prince. They crowded around him, banging him on his back roughly.

Prince shook the hands of the boys and girls surrounding him, then stepped over to where Roman stood all alone, watching the group of teenagers. As Prince held his hand out towards Roman, his mind went back into the past. It had been over four years since they had parted company. On that occasion they had been locked up in the bullpen in the city jail, each man sunk deep in his own thoughts. Both of them were aware that neither one of them would likely get out for a long time. They had been caught red-handed, with a car full of stolen television sets.

"Glad to see you, Prince," Roman said softly, his black eyes flashing with concealed amusement. He was medium in size, just under six feet, with slim, boyish shoulders. What caught the attention immediately was his keen features. His sharp nose was set off by the constant sneer on his tightly clenched lips.

In height, Prince towered over him. As the two men stared at each other, Prince held his hawklike eyes on Roman until the smaller man dropped his eyes. "Did you take care of everything like I told you to, Roman?" he asked quietly.

"Everything's been taken care of, Prince. We've just been waiting for you to get out so we can really stretch out."

Prince smiled slightly. Neither man spoke further until they left the station and entered the parking lot. One of the girls screamed sharply, then began to curse loudly.

"Goddamnit, Joan, can't you act like a young lady instead of some fuckin' whore who happened to be out for the night?" Roman yelled over his shoulder at the cursing woman. "You bitches can't go nowhere without cussing like goddamn fools."

"Prince," she called, "this sonofabitch here should be locked up in a goddamn cage somewhere." She pointed her finger at one of the members of the gang who was bringing up the rear.

Brute, the man she pointed out, grinned broadly. "Her ass is softer than cotton candy," he said loudly, to the amusement of his friends.

She stopped and pulled her sweater up, then removed a large knife from her bra. With a well-practiced, swift motion she pointed it towards Brute. "You put your fuckin' hands under my dress again, Brute, and I'll cut some of that fat off your lard-ass."

"Don't tell me a friendly little feel goin' cost Brute some of his ass?" one of the other members remarked, as they joked back and forth.

Joan, a tall, underweight, light-brown-skinned woman, kept up a steady flow of curse words until they reached the cars. She was pretending to be more angry than she actually was. Most of the men in the gang had had her at one time or another. What she really hoped to do was impress Prince. Knowing that he had just come home from prison, she hoped that he would end up spending the night with her. It would really be a feather in her cap if she could bed down with the big man. In her daydreams she could see herself as his number-one girl. She stared at his broad back as they stood beside the cars. She preferred tall black men, and Prince fit the bill perfectly. To her, he was the most handsome man she had ever seen.

Roman opened the door to a beat-up '62 Ford. "We ain't got but the two cars, baby, but I know things are going to change now that you're back home." He nodded towards the older car parked beside the Ford.

Joan forced her way into the car with Roman and Prince, pushing ahead of the two other girls who were trying to get in with them.

"The rest of you broads get in the other car," Roman ordered, after three girls climbed into the backseat. Everyone wanted to be close to Prince, the women most of all.

"Damn, baby," Roman exclaimed, "it seems as if all the bitches got hot pants for you, Prince. When your old lady gets out, she's goin' have big fun kickin' these back-stabbing bitches in the ass."

"Yeah man, they ain't never had no cherry before, and they think this is a cherry they'll be getting," Prince replied and laughed. He tossed his arm over the front car seat.

Roman, sitting between Prince and the driver, moved slightly to avoid his arm. "I should have put one of the broads up front," he said.

Shortman, a muscular, narrow-faced man, drove expertly, taking most of the side streets to avoid the downtown traffic. He turned on Michigan Avenue and followed it on out until he reached the slums. It was swarming with Mexicans, Italians, and other foreigners. Shortman slowed down in the worst part of the slum quarters and parked in front of the Roost.

The Roost was the main clubhouse of the Rulers, the best organized and most vicious young gang of teenagers Detroit had ever encountered. After convicting Prince and sending him to the state penitentiary, the police department's vice squad had made the blunder of thinking they had broken up this highly organized gang. After months of crime, the rumors began to come in that Prince was still running the organization, even though it was from behind prison walls.

Prince, waving right and left, led the way down the cellar steps into the Roost. Music blasted out of the open door. The couches along the walls were occupied by young couples locked in each other's arms. At the end of the room, ten young men wearing identical outfits were sitting on soft stools beside a long bar watching a girl swing her hips along with the beat of the music.

One of the men at the bar spotted Prince weaving through the crowd. He rose, walked over to the wall, and hit the light switch, flooding the room with light. A low mutter of discontent welled up, only to die down as Prince put his hands on his hips.

"If there's anybody in here who's not a gang leader," he said loudly, "step outside until after this meeting is over." Some of the fellows sitting by the wall began to leave, followed by their girls. Two of the men sitting at the bar stood up.

Prince waved them down. "All the members of the Rulers stay," he ordered. He waited until the door closed behind the last lagging person.

"Okay," he began, looking out over the still crowded room, "now we can get down to business. I guess all of you already know just about what I'm going to say, but you're not really hep to what the rewards are going to be. I hope that by the end of this week each of you will have your own private car for business and pleasure alike. From here on nobody makes a move without the okay of their district leader." He stopped speaking to make sure everyone was paying attention. "Before, you guys were fighting over such small things as what turfs or blocks each gang ruled. That kid shit is out." His voice carried the conviction that he wouldn't accept any interference. "In case any of you studs out there with twenty or thirty punks in your gang should happen to think you're a little too strong to have to take orders, look around you."

Slowly, Prince lit a cigarette. "Each man and woman here has at least ten followers in his gang. For those of you who can't count too goddamn good, there's at least sixty people here, not counting the broads, so that would be about six hundred studs. Are there any comments?"

"Yeah," a tall redheaded boy said. "If we can't make a score when we want to, man, how in the hell are we going to make our pocket money?"

"Don't worry!" Prince replied. "After today all of you are on my payroll. Each gang leader will receive fifty dollars for every ten members in his or her club."

"Say man," one of the guys yelled from the back suspiciously, "just what the hell we going to have to do for this money?"

"Don't worry," Prince assured him, "you won't have to do no more than what you've been doing. The only difference is that this time you'll be organized."

"Well, Prince, what about us?" one of the girls asked.

"The same goes for the women. You won't be called on to do much more than you're already doing."

"Just what do you mean," a slim girl standing on the side asked, "by too much more?"

"From here on out," Prince answered abruptly, "anytime one of you girls becomes strung out on drugs, we'll find a whorehouse for you to work out of before some pimp gets his hands on you. Also, whenever you find out one of the debs in your gang is screwing everybody and everything, that's whorehouse material, and the organization wants to know about it." He stared coldly at the women until they looked away.

"Now," Prince said softly, "there's one more thing you had better know. From here on out, whenever you see someone wearing one of these outfits," he turned and pointed at the outfits his gang members wore, "you can spread the word that there is going to be a hit made somewhere in this city. Other than that," he added significantly, "you'll never see them wear anything but silks or sport clothes."

He waited until he was sure they understood what he meant, then continued. "We're going to start an organization that almost every one of us in this room will sooner or later take a part in. All of you are aware of the rising cry of the sixties—'Black is Beautiful.' Well, we are going to jump on the grandstand with all the rest of the organizations that use this as their rallying cry. Before the month is out, we'll be backing a group of our own called 'F.N.L.M.' Those letters will mean 'Freedom Now Liberation Movement.' Behind that organization we'll be able to manipulate a whole lot of squares that ordinarily wouldn't go along with our program."

Prince removed a handkerchief and wiped the sweat from his brow. "There's no reason now for me to explain to you why we need this front or what we are going to do with it. All you need to know is that one day soon we'll be behind it."

He dropped his cigarette on the floor and stepped on it. "I haven't run down everything yet, but whatever else I've got to say to you, I'll get in touch with you over the phone. Sometime tomorrow the person who will be giving you your orders will stop by each of your clubhouses and you can get your questions answered completely."

Turning his back on the crowd, Prince said wearily, "I want all the members of the Rulers to meet me at my apartment within the next hour."

He turned abruptly and started through the crowd, followed by some of his more intimate friends. Behind him, a murmur of subdued voices whispered back and forth. It was as though a giant had just left their presence.

3

PRINCE STOPPED ON the sidewalk, inhaled the fresh evening air, and let his eyes rove over a couple of the young miniskirted girls as they passed by. They flirted with him boldly, switching their firm hips. Prince continued to watch them as they walked down the street. He hoped the short skirts would stay in style for another two or three years.

"I'll be damn glad when Ruby gets out," Prince said sharply. The sight of the girls had aroused his desire more than he wanted to admit.

"They gave her ten days last week for driving without a goddamn license," Shortman replied quickly, not aware that it was about the hundredth time someone had told Prince the same thing that day.

"She should get out Friday, Prince, if she don't

go and fuck up some kind of way," Roman added as he came up behind them.

Prince turned and glanced over his shoulder. Most of the members of the Rulers had come out of the club to form a crowd behind him.

"Well, let's get over to my place before we get picked up for loitering," Prince said and laughed pleasantly. Before the words were out of his mouth, young men and women began to pile into cars up and down the street. The elite of the gang scampered for seats in the car with Prince and Roman.

Brute, Fatdaddy, and Apeman used a flying wedge to monopolize the backseat. Danny, a vicious-natured young man in his early twenties, got in under the steering wheel.

Prince squeezed in the front seat between Roman and the driver, then twisted around. "What's been happening, Apeman? You look like you're trying to catch up with Fatdaddy in pounds," Prince said and grinned at the dark-skinned, hairy-armed man. Apeman, huge and brutal, grinned back. On his wide face the grin looked like a sneer, but it wasn't. He had been dedicated to Prince ever since grade school. There was a bond between them that Apeman held dear.

Among the three large men in the backseat of the car there was a constant challenge over which was the roughest. Fatdaddy might have exceeded the other two men by a few pounds, but when it came to viciousness, they were equal.

As the car moved away from the curb, Prince settled back in his seat and fell silent, thinking over some things that Roman had said to him earlier. He had spent four years planning, so Roman's objections were nothing new to him.

Prince spoke his thoughts out loud. "I didn't just start thinking about this thing, Roman. I been kicking your objections around, man, and I can see where you're coming from. I know when things get rough somebody is going to talk, but by the time we get finished with whoever does talk, it will be quite a while before somebody else tries to snitch on us again."

Danny gave a sharp bark that went for a laugh. "Yeah, baby, if there's one thing a nigger fears, it's the thought of someone sticking a blade between his shoulder blades." His harsh laughter sounded again. To people who did not know him, it would have been a chilling sound. But to these men who lived beside him, he was just being himself. They all knew that he was a dangerous man, but they considered themselves just as dangerous, if not more so.

Roman laughed. "What are you going to use to enforce this fear, Prince," he asked sardonically, "the fearsome three sitting in the backseat?"

Brute spoke up. "I don't see what's so goddamn funny about that, Roman. You ain't the big wheel in the show no more, so be cool. Prince might give us the go-ahead and you'll see just how efficient we can be."

"Sweet Jesus!" Danny exclaimed. "I wouldn't mind helping out the fearsome three if that's the case."

Roman frowned at Danny. "You better keep your lip buttoned, punk," he said, "or you might find yourself unable to close it."

With a casual gesture, Danny removed a straight razor from his pocket. "The only reason I've followed you up to now, Roman," he said, "is because I've had my orders from Prince; other than that, boy, I'd have stuck my razor in your ass long ago."

The roar of laughter from the backseat caused Prince to intervene. "Okay, killer," he said coldly, "all of you will get a chance to show your best hands before it's over, so be cool."

The group in the car fell silent. Prince reflected on his closest men as the silence held. Roman was a good man, smart, but he lacked the ruthlessness it took to rule such a gang. When they had been in the city jail waiting to go before the judge, it was Roman who had come up with the idea of flipping a coin to see who would take the weight. Prince lost, so he had pleaded guilty, stating that Roman had accepted a lift not knowing that the stuff in the backseat of the car was stolen.

It had been doubtful whether or not the judge believed him, but they realized that if Prince stuck with his testimony, it would have been impossible to convict Roman, so they released him.

"What's this black power bit, baby?" Danny asked suddenly.

"You should know as well as I do," Prince replied. "With all this black awareness coming to light, we're going to ride to the top of the hill on it. Once we get organized, we'll be able to function smoother and faster. I was in the joint when all that burning and looting jumped off in '67, but I'm here now. With the organization we're fixing to start, we'll be able to sway the people, start fights against the Man. Keep pounding it into the people's faces about police brutality, which there's always plenty of. All we got to do is keep it before the people's faces, and every time the pigs do something to a black man that stinks, we'll be on the case and cash in on it."

Danny hesitated briefly, then said, "I don't like the idea of frontin' our people off, Prince. They catch too much hell already without us stickin' a dick to them."

"We ain't goin' front them off, baby," Prince replied quickly. "If anything, we'll be showing them the way. Today is the year of the black man's revolution. Whenever a revolution jumps off, somebody gains, so why not us during this particular one?"

Danny pulled up and parked in front of a row of apartments that resembled modern motel cabins.

"This joint here," Roman began, "is the best. . . ."

"Knock it off," Prince interrupted. "I don't want no excuses. If this is the pad you copped for me, it's too late now for you to start trying to clean up;

211

BLACK GANGSTER

you should have thought about it and handled it before I came home."

They entered the dinky apartment single file. Prince glanced around at the cheap furniture. The end tables were burned from cigarettes left carelessly around.

"Roman," Prince said softly, "do you really think all the members can fit into this death trap?"

Roman laughed self-consciously. "Yeah, man. They can all get in here. I would have gotten something bigger but, man, I just didn't have that kind of bread."

Cars began to pull up in front of the house, and the first group to arrive called back and forth to friends in other cars. The few girls mixed in the arriving crowds squealed loudly as they came in the door. Brute, standing beside the door, was giving everyone in a skirt a pinch on the rear.

The room quickly filled with whispering, laughing teenagers. Prince slowly raised his hand for silence. Immediately, the room became as quiet as a tomb.

Roman, watching, fought back his anger. After being the leader of this gang for over four years, he still couldn't command that kind of respect.

Prince pulled up a chair and propped his foot on it. "All right," he said quietly, "let's get down to business. I've already split up the districts that each of you will collect from. If any of you should run into any trouble trying to collect any money, contact Roman, Danny, or Chinaman."

Donald Goines

"Collect the money from who?" Shortman asked, dumbfounded.

Prince glanced around the room, noticing the puzzlement on the faces staring at him. "Each of you will collect your money from the people that attended the meeting tonight at the club. They in turn will collect theirs from all the business places in their districts."

"That sounds like the old extortion bit, Prince. Ain't that just about been wore out?" one of the members asked.

"Yeah, it's been used time and time again, but not the way we are going to do it. There ain't enough pigs on the police force to handle all the trouble we goin' send their way. Sometime tomorrow, Brute, Apeman, Fatdaddy, and a few more of you will pay a surprise visit to most of the business places in the inner city. It don't make no difference if it's owned by black or white, they all get the same treatment."

Prince pulled a cigarette from his pack and tossed the empty package on the floor. "After you begin tearing the place up," he continued, "I'll send the gang from the neighborhood around to stop you. Now, if the storekeepers don't get the message, we'll just put his or her John Henry in our little black book and when we pay our next visit, they'll never forget it, 'cause we'll be playing for keeps."

"Damn, Prince," one of the members said, "they'll have so many policemen there when we go back, you won't be able to see past the god-damn uniforms."

"Don't worry about the cops," Prince replied. "They won't be able to stay there forever, and we got all the time in the world to wait. I got one of the best young lawyers in the country, so we won't have to worry about any bullshit arrests. As long as we got plenty money on hand bond won't be any problem. In case someone should take a fall, though, they won't have any worries. We'll take care of their people for them as long as they're away, plus put up a large nest-egg for them so that when they get out they'll have some nice money waiting."

Prince waited until he thought his words had sunk in before continuing. "Our largest income will come from dope and corn whiskey. I've already picked out which of you will be my collectors on the drugs being sold in this city. After tomorrow not a drop of horse, dexies, or reefer will be sold in this town without us getting some part of the money. All the dealers will have to pay protection to operate."

Again he waited to see the effect of his words. "I know a lot of you don't know anything about corn whiskey," he said as he removed a small notebook from his back pocket, "but it's big business." He flipped open a page. "Last year alone, in Detroit, there was over five million dollars made off of homemade whiskey."

It was a staggering sum to most of the young people in the room. They whispered back and forth until Prince interrupted. "That's right, five million, and here in this city, it's a black man's racket. Now, what we're going to do is monopolize the whiskey business. In three months, if we can get big enough, not a drop of whiskey will be sold unless we make it."

Roman stepped up beside Prince, a small notebook in his hand. "So far, we got eight whiskey stills ready to be put up, plus all the corn and sugar we'll need." He ran his finger down the page. "We got six houses rented, with the stills inside the house, waiting for operators. As far as customers go, we got fifty customers who'll take from twenty gallons down to five gallons from us at a time."

Prince nodded his head, pleased. "Homemade whiskey brings ten dollars a gallon, or if the customer buys over twenty gallons at a time, we'll let it go for eight dollars a gallon." Prince read from his notebook. "Shortman will be in charge of the operation. He will have four of you as his lieutenants. Each one of you will have a district. Your job will be to see that the members of whatever gangs are assigned to you produce enough whiskey to keep your side of the city up until we can get more stills in operation." Prince stopped and flipped a page. "Each still should be able to produce at least thirty gallons of whiskey a day. In seven days your quota will be no less than two hundred and ten gallons. At ten dollars a jug, you can add it up yourself and see how much money we'll be making."

Prince's plan had left the people in the apartment stunned. At first, his ideas had been unbelievable to most of them, but the longer he talked, the more the magnetism of his personality won them over.

"Tess," Prince said, speaking to a tall brown-skinned girl wearing a high natural, "I want you to take over absolute control of all the debs until Ruby is released. Your main job will be to see that most of the girls take at least two tricks a night someplace where the boys can roll them without too much trouble. Danny will be working right beside you, so you won't have too much to worry about. The main thing is that, as soon as your girls lead a trick off, you make damn sure that girl gets the hell out of that neighborhood."

"That," Danny said, "don't seem like too much of a job to me, just taking off some drunk chasing his hard around."

Prince laughed harshly. "Don't worry," he said, "there's more to it than that. We're going to need as many stolen cars as we can get for various jobs. Sometimes when we have a large job on hand, you'll have to detain some poor trick while the boys borrow his papers to go along with his car."

Danny laughed. His admiration for Prince was obvious. "Yeah, man, I can dig it now. Just keep the trick under wraps until after the sting goes off."

"That's right, baby," Prince replied. "You got the picture now. Whatever men you might need, just let me or Roman know, and you can have them."

Prince glanced around at all the astonished faces. The magnitude of his plans had jolted them out of their fantasies of toughness.

"I didn't bother telling you," Prince said, his voice harsh, "but it goes without saying: there's no such thing as quitting. You're all in it 'til the bitter end—if it should happen to go that way."

Preacher, a tall brown-skinned Negro wearing a midnight-black silk suit, stood up. He casually displayed the exquisite jewelry on his wrist with a swift motion of his left arm. "Prince," he began, "I'm having a little trouble down in the Hastings projects."

"Oh! And how is that?" Prince asked.

"Well, to begin with," Preacher said, "everybody here is hip to the stud I'm having trouble with. The stud thinks he's a little too big for this thing you're trying to work out of, Prince. He also told me to tell you not to come down in the projects with that shit of yours, 'cause he don't want to hear it."

Prince studied Preacher coldly. "How many guys does he have following him now?"

"I'd say he's got at least a hundred, if not more."

"If something happened to Dave, Preacher, who would fill his shoes?" Prince asked softly.

"That's easy," Preacher replied. "You're lookin' at him right now."

"Can I depend on that?" Prince asked softly.

"You can damn well depend on it, Prince. Once Dave is out of the way, I'll be the big dog down there."

The meaning of the conversation was not missed by anybody in the room. Everybody knew that Square Dave was big not only in his own neighborhood but anywhere in the city he chose to go.

A young girl with hair bleached bright blonde yelled, "Say, Prince, when are we going to start celebrating your homecoming?"

"Soon, honey, soon, but first we're going to take care of the business at hand," Prince said sharply. "So, first of all, I want all of you to put your Ruler outfits on, and then I want you to make sure you're seen all over the city."

"That means there's going to be trouble in the city, don't it, Prince?" Shortman asked.

"You hit the nail on the head, baby boy, that's just what it means," Prince replied. "Make sure all of you have an airtight alibi. Stay in the lights wherever you've taken a notion to be. Make sure you're seen, but make sure you can prove where you were at, too."